Jinsen

As he got closer and I got a look at his face, I saw that he looked perfectly normal, except that he was smiling. Not a nervous smile, or that tight bottled-up grin you get when you're really humiliated and trying not to show it; no, it was a real sunny regular all's-right-with-the-world smile, which meant that he was either high, or crazy. Or—

—closer now, coming right up to our table, big ears and tilted, sleepy eyes, not bald but shaved, you could see the blond stubble poking up on his scalp. But you could tell he wasn't a skinhead, or anything sick like that, just—just *strange*, the way a platypus is strange, or one of those deep-sea plants, waving waxy fingers on the ocean floor. "Excuse me," he said to us, very politely. "Do you have any change?"

"What's the matter?" I asked. "Forget your lunch money?"

His smile went wider still; for a second I thought of Humpty-Dumpty, that bald head smiling all around itself as "Oh no," he said. "I'm begging. Like a monk, you know?"

OTHER SPEAK BOOKS YOU MAY ENJOY

KATHE KOJA

Buddha Boy

speak

An Imprint of Penguin Group (USA) Inc.

SPEAK

Published by the Penguin Group

Penguin Group (USA) Inc., 345 Hudson Street, New York, New York 10014, U.S.A.

Penguin Group (Canada), 10 Alcorn Avenue, Toronto, Ontario, Canada M4V 3B2
(a division of Pearson Penguin Canada Inc.)

Penguin Books Ltd, 80 Strand, London WC2R 0RL, England

Penguin Ireland, 25 St Stephen's Green, Dublin 2, Ireland
(a division of Penguin Books Ltd)

Penguin Group (Australia), 250 Camberwell Road, Camberwell, Victoria 3124,
Australia (a division of Pearson Australia Group Pty Ltd)

Penguin Books India Pvt Ltd, 11 Community Centre, Panchsheel Park,
New Delhi - 110 017, India

Penguin Group (NZ), Cnr Airborne and Rosedale Roads, Albany, Auckland,
New Zealand (a division of Pearson New Zealand Ltd)

Penguin Books (South Africa) (Pty) Ltd, 24 Sturdee Avenue, Rosebank,
Johannesburg 2196, South Africa

Registered Offices: Penguin Books Ltd, 80 Strand, London WC2R 0RL, England

First published in the United States of America by Frances Foster Books,
Farrar, Straus and Giroux, 2003

Published by Speak, an imprint of Penguin Group (USA) Inc., 2004

1 3 5 7 9 10 8 6 4 2

LIBRARY OF CONGRESS CATALOGING-IN-PUBLICATION DATA

Koja, Kathe.
Buddha boy / Kathe Koja.
p. cm.
Summary: Justin spends time with Jinsen, the unusual and artistic new student
whom the school bullies torment and call Buddha Boy, and ends up making
choices that impact Jinsen, himself, and the entire school.

ISBN 0-14-240209-5 (pbk.)

[1. Conduct of life—Fiction. 2. Peer pressure—Fiction. 3. Artists – Fiction.
4. Buddhism—Fiction. 5. High schools—Fiction. 6. Schools—Fiction.
7. Orphans—Fiction.] I. Title. PZ7.K8312Bu 2004 [Fic]—dc22 2004041669

Printed in the United States of America

For Rick and Aaron

*My thanks to Rick Lieder, Aaron Mustamaa,
Frances Foster, and Chris Schelling, for all their help*

Buddha
Boy

One

Like a flashback memory, he's there in my mind: skimming up the stairs at school, his sloppy old T-shirt big as a sail, red tie-dyed dragon T-shirt, who wears stuff like that? No one. Jinsen. Head turned and laughing at something someone had said, to him? at him? I don't know. Once McManus called him a human lint ball, and he laughed about it all day.

Him going up, me down below, he saw me and waved and "Later," he called down, "I'll tell you everything." And he did, too, but by then I already knew.

Karma, it was all karma. Just don't ask me what that really means.

———

If you didn't notice the name—red letters on the side of the gym, a red lion crouching over: EDWARD RUCHER HIGH

SCHOOL, HOME OF THE PRIDE—you'd say, *Oh, that must be a prison.* Three faceless stories of black reflector windows, beige brick all over like the builders got it cheap, but inside everything is expensive and new: the computers in the Media Center, the carpeting in the hallways, the sparkling white tile in the Olympic-sized pool. It's the kind of school where the kids are always bitching about parking permits because they all have their own cars. New cars, and credit cards, and all the money they want for partying at the Barn.

I don't hang out at the Barn, I don't have a credit card, I eat in the cafeteria instead of going out to McDonald's or Pizza Ray's. It's not like we can't afford that stuff, or most of it anyway, but Audrey—my mother—says it's all unnecessary. Love, nature, music (especially jazz music): to her, those are *necessary.* But national-debt sneakers and spring break in Cancún? Forget it. She thinks most of the kids at Rucher are growing up seriously deluded, and she's determined that I'm not going to be the same way.

How about just a little deluded? Just enough to have a new car?

It's not funny, Justin. Those poor kids are screwed up.

I admit, some of them really are. But it wasn't so much the money as the way the money made them act: like if you

4

can buy pretty much anything you want, you start thinking you can do pretty much anything you want. Like McManus and his crew: Magnur, and Josh Winston, and Hooks. Kings of the school, strutting around like they were characters in a movie, the cool guys, the bad-good guys, the ones everybody wants to be. You were supposed to be grateful or something if McManus noticed you, or bummed a cigarette off you, or made a crappy joke about your clothes—

Justin, man, nice sweater. Knit it yourself?

—but I mostly just ignored him and his jokes, like I ignored the whole social-status in-out thing, or at least as much of it as I could. Like a set of laws you didn't make and don't agree with but have to abide by anyway, laws that specify who you can be with, who you can talk to, who you have to ignore or face the penalty of being ignored yourself, if not something worse. Our little group—we'd been buddies since middle school, Jakob and Megan and me—was mostly somewhere in the middle, never invited to the big-deal parties but not exiled to the outer limits, either. It's not a bad place to be, the middle: it's comfortable, it's easy, and it's safe. And I'd probably still be there if it wasn't for Jinsen.

———

"*What* is *that*?" from Megan in her usual drama-queen way: but it was a sight, really, this skinny bald-headed kid in

5

a size million T-shirt, backpack humped and lumpy as a turtle's shell, making his way across the cafeteria like a rabbit crossing the freeway: this way, that way, looking all around. "An *exchange* student? From *Mars*?"

"No, they only come in the fall," said Jakob, taking one of my fries. "Like last year, that one girl, where was she from? Latvia? Estonia?"

"You mean the one with the *braids*," Megan said, mock-shuddering. "Once in gym class, she was doing these back-flips, and her braids got caught on the—Justin, *what* are you staring at?"

"I'm trying to figure out what he's doing," because I was, because it didn't make any sense: going from table to table, asking for something? but wherever he went people stared at him, laughed at him, one of McManus's crew threw something at him, a pencil? a straw? and the whole table howled when he stooped to pick it up and bring it back. For a second I wondered if he was a Special Needs kid, but Special Needs don't have the same lunch hour as we do, and anyway almost nobody picks on them.

Then as he got closer and I got a look at his face, I saw that he wasn't Special Needs at all, he looked perfectly normal, except that he was smiling. Not a nervous smile, or that tight bottled-up grin you get when you're really humiliated and trying not to show it; no, it was a real sunny regular all's-right-with-the-world smile, which meant that he was either high, or crazy. Or—

—closer now, coming right up to our table, big ears and tilted, sleepy eyes, not bald but shaved, you could see the blond stubble poking up on his scalp. But you could tell he wasn't a skinhead, or anything sick like that, just—just *strange*, the way a platypus is strange, or one of those deep-sea plants, waving waxy fingers on the ocean floor. "Excuse me," he said to us, very politely. "Do you have any change?"

"*What*?" said Megan in spite of herself, then looked away, mortified that she'd said anything at all, that she'd even acknowledged this kid standing there with his hand out, even the biggest moochers didn't go about it as blatantly as this. "What's the matter?" I asked. "Forget your lunch money?"

His smile went wider still; for a second I thought of Humpty-Dumpty, that bald head smiling all around itself as "Oh no," he said. "I'm begging. Like a monk, you know?"

"Like a what?" but Megan gave me a glare you could have used to cut metal, *Don't talk to the weirdo* because people were staring at us now, staring and snickering. "Here," I said, digging in my pocket, handing him a dollar and "Thanks," he said, and moved off to the next table where one of the basketball jocks was waiting with a can of Mountain Dew. He must have shaken it up first because as soon as the bald kid put out his hand Jocko sprayed him, wet spurt all over his shirt, big laughs but not from me because I didn't think it was funny, all Jocko had to do was say no. "What an asshole," I said, but "Exactly," Megan nodded, folding her arms. "*Everyone* was looking. *Don't* do it again."

Before the lunch bell I left to hustle up to Econ, needing to finish yesterday's worksheet on the Federal Reserve—is there anything more boring than worksheets? or economics? Maybe watching dust form. People started filing in, I was almost done, and "Hey," from the kid who sits behind me, Tim Elder, he always smells like menthol cigarettes. "Here comes the alien, man. You see what he did at lunch?"

And sure enough it was the monk-boy, bald head, drenched T-shirt and all, talking to Ms. Keller, who handed him a book, pointed him toward a seat as the bell went off (actually it's not a bell, it's a tone, like the ones they have in prisons), and as he passed me he smiled, just a little, not the way you smile at someone you don't know but kind of do— like the mailman, say, or the counter guy at 7-Eleven—but the way you catch the eye of a friend you didn't expect to see: *Hey, hi, I didn't think you'd be here.*

And I felt myself—why?—wanting to smile back, I almost did but then of course I didn't because of course Megan was right, there was no point in making friends with someone like that, no point in even pretending, so I looked back down at my worksheet until he had passed and didn't think about him again till after school, till "Hey," Jakob said, sunglasses on, inching out of the student parking lot in his dad's gray minivan; it was his turn to drive today. "There's your friend, Justin. Buddha Boy."

Tramping through the slush, hands in pockets, backpack even bigger than before, as if his whole life were crammed inside, and "*Look* at him," Megan said, as if this were the best evidence yet of his weirdness. "It's like 20 degrees out, and he's not even *wearing* a *coat.*"

"Buddha Boy?"

"That's what McManus is calling him."

As we passed I looked at him, not so he could see, but he wasn't looking at me anyway, he was focused on where he was going, straight ahead. "Maybe monks don't wear coats," I said.

"He is not a monk," Megan said, clearly enunciating each word for my benefit. "He is a feeb. A bald feeb.—Go to

Cuppa Jane's," to Jakob as we pulled into traffic. "I *have* to get a cappuccino."

———

Ms. Keller—people call her "Killer Keller"—has long lean fingers and even longer nails, dragon-lady nails lacquered a deadly pink; when she points at you, you know it. So when she started pointing out partners for some big new "creative" project, I stopped doodling in my notebook and paid attention.

"—Andy and Luis, Laura and Kelly and Leah, Justin and Tim and—and Michael Martin," nodding to the monk-slash-alien as Tim Elder dug hard into my back: "No way he's our partner, man," too loud but I totally agreed: I wasn't wild about Menthol Tim, either, but at least he and I were on the same side of that invisible divide, the normal vs. the—well, the not-normal, the outcasts and the strange, the ones like Buddha Boy (although there wasn't anyone quite like him, he was kind of in a class by himself, sitting there in his dragon T-shirt, bubbled and peeling from too many trips to the dryer). "You have to say something to her," Tim's urgent mutter. "You have to get us out of this."

"Why me? Why can't you talk to her?" but in the end he just stood beside her desk like a statue and left me to do the dirty work, try to explain why we didn't want Buddha Boy for a partner: "He's, he's new," I said, sounding lame even to myself. "And he doesn't know anything about what we've been doing in class—"

"The projects are self-explanatory," Keller said. "And you two can help him." I looked at Tim, Tim stared at the floor, and "Some kids," she said, a cool and seamless gaze, steepling those long pink nails, "have been pretty mean to him already, because he's kind of—different. I know I can count on you not to do that."

Which, translated, meant *I know exactly what your problem is and I have no sympathy,* so back we went to our seats, where I sat for the rest of the hour quietly writing SHIT SHIT SHIT in the margins of my notebook, as across the aisle Buddha Boy (had he heard us?) scratched busily away, taking notes? drawing? who knows. I didn't look at him again until the bell rang, up from my seat and eager to get away but there he was, like a stray you can't get rid of, standing right in the aisle, right by my desk and "Justin?" in that same polite voice. "I guess we're going to work to-gether?"

"I guess."

He held out the projects list. "Do you want to do the, the board-game thing? It looks like it might be fun."

Make a board game illustrating an economic principle, in-cluding a three-page paper explaining the game: fun, right. "Sure," I said, hoping no one was watching us, wishing he

11

would get out of my way—but for all his bald-headed politeness he was determined, he was going to pin me down to a time and place, so "How about tomorrow," I said, "at, at your house?" figuring no one I knew would be in the vicinity, and I could get in and out without anyone seeing me—except Tim Elder, who had conveniently vanished as Michael Martin/Buddha Boy scratched down the coordinates, directions, address. "I get home around five, I'll see you then."

"Sure," again like it was the only word I knew. "I'll be there," with my good buddy Tim Elder, who I finally cornered in the bathroom, having a cigarette break but "No way," he said when I told him. "I'm not going over to his house."

"You have to. You heard Keller, we're stuck with him."

"No," blowing smoke, *"you're* stuck with him. I'll just take the F. I'm getting a B+ anyway, one project won't hurt me that much." But it would hurt me, already I was a low C, barely getting by and even if I didn't care Audrey would, so "Thanks a lot," I said, and banged out the door, almost late, now, to Art, thinking as I hustled down the emptying hall, *We'll get the thing started, I'll take it home with me and finish it, and I'll never have to talk to him again. Or Tim Elder, either.*

Two

Do you know the concept of karma? It's kind of like a circle, or cause-and-effect, like a slow-tolling bell you rang maybe a year ago, five years ago, maybe in another lifetime if you believe in that. Karma means that what you do today, and why you do it, makes you who you are forever: as if you were clay, and every thought and action left a mark in that clay, bent it, shaped it, even ruined it . . . but with karma there are no excuses, no explanations, no I-didn't-really-mean-it-so-can-I-have-some-more-clay. Karma takes everything you do very, very seriously.

———

I like Art. It's an easy B for me, sometimes even an A if I'm really rolling, and it's the one place in school where I actually get to be creative. And I like the art teacher, too, probably the best of all my teachers. Mr. Snell (also known as Mr. Smell, for the turpentine odor that follows him around like a dog) is usually pretty cool: he lets us play the radio as loud as we want, he doesn't get mad if you screw up supplies, in fact the only thing you can do to really fail his class is not to try at all.

That day we were starting on scroll paintings: a long tongue of watercolor paper, painted up and down with ideograms, Japanese words copied from the corkboard at the front of the room. McManus and Josh Winston were making a big deal out of the fact that the words were in another language, asking Snell in this fake-worried way what would happen if they copied it wrong and wrote *bite me* instead of, say, *hello* or *good luck*. "Or, like, 'go to hell,' " McManus said, smirking. "Or 'kiss my big red'—well. You know."

A bunch of junior girls snickered, Megan made a face: "That's McAnus for you," but I don't mind that stuff so much. What I hate is that McManus thinks—believes—that he's the best artist in the class, like it's some divine right he has, to be the best at everything there is. Which he's not.

But Snell doesn't fall for that kind of stuff. "If you're worried about what the words mean," he said, "check the translation sheet. There's one on every table. In English," he added, as if he were trying to be helpful, but with a little bit of a smile to show them he knew what was what.

I hadn't even glanced at the sheet, I didn't care what the words actually meant. I was just going for the feel, the swirl and pattern of it, the way the symbols moved and climbed atop each other like alien creatures at play. It's how my dad taught me to look at art.

He's an artist himself, a painter who works mostly with oils to make square, spare abstract paintings, some big as the wall of a room; he paints and paints all day, then some-times sleeps in his studio, so he can work at night if he wakes up and gets the urge. He doesn't live with me and Audrey, they got divorced when I was small, but he and I keep in pretty close touch.

He's a good dad, but he's really . . . different. When I was a kid, he used to send me all these books about art, which completely aggravated me: I wanted Nintendo for my birth-day, not Picasso. Then I got a little older and started actually looking at the books. I'll never be an artist, but I've learned to appreciate being able to really see what's going on in a painting, or a piece of sculpture. *Use your eyes,* my dad al-ways says. *It's amazing what happens when you do.*

Now "Nice work, Justin," said Snell, pausing behind me

to watch for a minute. "You know this one here—" tapping one of the ideograms, "is a symbol for 'mindfulness.' The top part, the little roof, means 'now.' The lower element means 'heart' and 'mind' together. It could be translated as 'being full-hearted, open-minded, right now.' "

"Really?" I said, even though I didn't care.

"Really," he said, and moved on.

———

"This is it," I said to Audrey. "Teresa Street, turn here." Hemmed in by my sack of art supplies (markers, X-Acto knife, foamcore board; with those mismatched clothes of his, who knew what Buddha Boy might have to work with, or if he had anything at all), I squinted through the windshield's snowy drizzle, looking for *302, gray-blue house with a garden out front*, which, if you consider two bald rosebushes and a dead potted mum a garden, was just about right. There was an old rust-dusted minivan in the gravel driveway, and no lights on in the house.

"Are you sure he's home?" Audrey asked.

"He said five o'clock," yesterday, though I hadn't talked to him today, had only seen him in passing before Econ, struggling with his locker, someone had probably jammed the door. Or glued the lock. For fun.

There are plenty of those little fun things to do—jamming

lockers, stealing lunches, hiding backpacks or books or gym clothes—before it tips over into bad stuff, the serious ass-kicking kind. Like last year in swim class, McManus and Magnur kept hassling this one kid, David Pink, holding him under water until he almost passed out, until the swim coach finally noticed what was going on and made them stop. Although according to McManus, he and Magnur and Pink were just "joking around"; yeah, right. Why they didn't suspend him I don't know, except that I do—Mark McManus, school god, how could he ever do anything really bad? And David Pink, freshman nobody, what could he do but keep his mouth shut before something worse happened to him? Magnur—some people call him "Cro-Magnur"—is built like a brick house. Which is one reason why Rucher was All-State in football last year. Which was what got Magnur off the hook, I guess.

Anyway, afterwards we had this big "sensitivity" assembly, and Mr. Valente—he's the principal—talked about how it was our differences as people that made us all strong, and then he made everybody sign the Peace Pledge, this big yellow poster that was supposed to symbolize our commitment to getting along, or something. David Pink signed it first, then McManus and Magnur, then all the rest of us, filing up in a row; it took forever, kids were signing *Mr. X* and

17

Mickey Mouse, intelligent stuff like that. When it was Jakob's turn he signed "Gandhi," which Megan thought was stupid, but I said it made just as much sense as signing the stupid Pledge in the first place. As if anything outside of us, like an assembly, would change what really went on inside and underneath. In was in and out was out and that was that.

Which was why I hadn't told Megan or Jakob where I was headed after school; I just said I had an appointment, which was true, right? I mean, I wasn't a total jerk like Tim Elder, but I didn't want the whole world to know, either. Even though it wasn't like we were hanging out together, Buddha Boy and me, it wasn't like I really had a choice.

Now "I don't think—" Audrey said, and "There he is," I said at the same time: trudging slowly down the street, back bent but head up, he raised one arm when he saw me in the car.

"He's not even wearing a *coat*," Audrey said, not like Megan had said it but the way a mom says it, like *This is an outrage!* "Is his family very poor, Justin? You've got that blue parka from last year, maybe we could give—"

"No," at once, my hand on the door, and I felt Audrey look at me, not a good look, as I stepped out of the car, right into a puddle, chill soak into my sock as "Hi," Buddha Boy said, slogging up. "Sorry I'm late."

18

I followed him up the porch steps. If my feet were cold his had to be freezing; his sweatshirt was practically stuck to his back, and "Where were you?" I said, to say something. "Did you have to stay after school, or—"

"No, I went to the temple,"—*what temple?*—and then he was unlocking the door, stepping into a dim, cramped living room, two plaid armchairs and a ruptured La-Z-Boy, after-scent of something sweet and burned. "You want a Coke or something?" he said as he led me into a kitchen much smaller and darker than ours, bent to turn on a space heater that gave off more sound than heat, a buzzing noise like a big captured bug. As I set down my plastic sack, he cleared the table—a square of newspapers and magazines; some mail; a squat glass bowl, its red glaze so glossy it looked wet, half-burnt sticks stuck in sand inside it. Incense, that was the smell.

"I had a couple of ideas already," he said, reaching into his sodden backpack to take out his math book, sketchbook, a handful of paper that he held out to me. "Tell me what you think."

As I took them I saw his hand was shaking, *he* was shaking, short quick shivers like a dog and I almost said something, then didn't, then blurted, "Why don't you ever wear a coat?" And immediately felt stupid, it wasn't any of my business, but "Discipline," he said; he was smiling a little,

19

like he was maybe glad I'd asked. "Like an athlete trains, you know?"

I didn't know; what kind of athlete trains by freezing? The Polar Bear Club? but then he left the room, left me with the Coke and the papers, so I sat down and started to read.

The purpose of this game is to CONSUME: to spend more money and buy more things than any other player, and become "King Consumer."

He'd made a sketch of how the board should look: every square a kind of store, and little people in each of the corners, all smiling, all wearing oversize crowns.

Each player receives money for passing "Go" and must spend it all on that trip around the board. Any money left over goes back into the bank.

He'd drawn cartoons in the margins, too: dollar signs, clothes on hangers, cars with radiating lines around them to show how new and shiny they were; and some little creatures who were round as balloons with small pinched-up mouths, I didn't know what they were supposed to be. The whole thing was actually pretty funny, how it seemed to be one thing but was really something else, like he was making fun of buying too much even though the whole game was about shopping—BIG SALE!!, THIS YEAR'S MODEL, SAVE

50%. The cartoons were pretty good, too, in fact they were very good, especially the people with the crowns, looking happy and sorry at once . . . and all of a sudden there he was, in a dry shirt, another dumb dragon, where did he get this stuff? Ye Olde Hippie Thrift Shoppe? "So," he said. "What do you think?"

"It's good," I said, "really good. Let's do it," and started getting my stuff out but "That's OK," he said, and reached under the table for a toolbox, a tackle box filled, I saw, with art supplies, really choice art supplies, even better than what we had at school. "I think there's enough here."

Expensive markers and mechanical pencils, wrong-size thrift store clothes, how did those things go together? But I didn't ask, just started sketching out the game board on the foamcore: "I'll rough it in, OK, and you can finish it off. . . . What are these?" pointing with my pencil at the balloon-figures. "What are they supposed to be?"

For a minute he didn't say anything, then "It's a Buddhist thing," with a little shrug. "We don't have to leave them in."

"No, it's OK. I just wondered what they were."

He looked at me as if he were trying to decide something, then shrugged again. "They're called *pretas*," he said. "Hungry ghosts. Big big bodies and little tiny mouths, they eat all the time but they never get full. Like when you have a lot of stuff, you have everything, but all you want is more."

Hungry ghosts; King Consumer—I had to smile, and he smiled too. "So you're, like, Buddhist or something? Like a monk, you said?" Which would explain the bald part, right? And maybe the no-coat stuff too.

He looked at me, head to one side, stubble glinting in the tired overhead light, and "Well," he said, then paused, as if he might say something else, but thought better of it. "I like Buddhism," he said, then started taking markers out of the tackle box, meaning the subject was pretty much closed.

Which was fine with me. I'm not a big religious-type person, Audrey drags me to church every year on Christmas Eve but that's about it. My dad is more into it; he used to belong to some kind of church, Protestant I guess, I remember us going to it a long, long time ago. Dark wood pews, stained-glass windows, singing along to the organ. . . . But we never go when I visit him now; I don't know why, we just don't.

The thing I never understood about religion is how it doesn't seem to make any difference. I mean, here all these people go to church all the time, and it never seems to go any deeper than that, I mean it doesn't make them better people or change the way they act in the real world or any-thing, so what good is it? Like what if McManus went to church (and maybe he does, for all I know)? You think he'd stop holding people under water, and calling them faggots, and stuff like that?

It was quiet in the kitchen; the space heater buzzed on, then off, then on again. I sat scratching away on the foam-core, slow and labored, until it occurred to me that he ought to be the one doing the sketching, seeing as he could draw about a hundred times better than I could so "Hey," I said, straightening up, "hey, Budd—" then stopped short, *oh good move* so I tried to make it sound like I was coughing or clearing my throat, why doesn't that ever work? and I tried again, "Hey, Michael," but that sounded weird too and anyway he shook his head, not mad, just to stop me getting any deeper. "My name," he said, "is Jinsen. My real name."

"Ginseng?"

"Jinsen," patient. "It's like a, a spiritual name, you know?"

"Yeah?" I said, because I didn't know what else to say, a spiritual name? what did that mean? so "What I was going to say was, you want to do the drawing? And I can write the paper," at home on my computer, not here in this dumpy kitchen where I just made a jerk of myself. "Sure," he said, and swiveled the foamcore his way, mechanical pencil in action, and in about ten minutes he had the whole thing sketched out, working fast but with no wasted motion, it was like watching a ballet dancer, or a surgeon, or an athlete, someone who's trained to do one thing and do it really well.

He started in on the lettering next, working in that same quick quiet way. He'd have the whole thing done in an hour so why was I even here? But Audrey wouldn't be back until seven and it was barely five after six, so for something to do I reached for his sketchbook, there on the pile of magazines, asking with a look *OK?* and "Sure," he said. "Tell me what you think."

The first page was blank, a calm off-white space; the second had a drawing of a tree. Just that, just a pen-and-ink tree, but it was—perfect. Not like a photograph, not "perfect" like "exact." It was definitely someone's drawing, but at the same time it *was* a tree—the way a tree *is*, the way the wind moves through its leaves, the rough skin of the bark, the shade it gives. . . . All this in about thirty lines, black on white. I'd never seen anything like it, not outside an art book, anyway.

And the rest of the pages were like that, too. Not only the look but the feel of the thing, whatever it was he was drawing: sailboats on a lake, a burning candle, two people walking on a faraway hill—when you saw the picture you were there, you were in it, you *were* it. "Hey," I said, "hey, this is *amazing*," but I wasn't even listening to myself, I was just looking, turning the pages—a broken bottle, the sky before a storm, a curtain half-pulled in a bedroom window and "Mostly," he said, "I just draw what there is," lettering KING CONSUMER! across the face of the foamcore, glancing up at me then down again. "You like art?"

"Yeah. Yeah I do. My dad's an artist, a painter—he would love this stuff.—Hey, you ever show this to Snell?"

"Who's Snell?"

"The art teacher. At school."

"I don't have Art," he said, which was unbelievable, anybody who could draw like this belonged in Art, anybody who could draw like this could teach the class. "That's crazy," I said, "you've got to get in there. . . . Like right now we're doing these scroll paintings, Japanese, you know? You could blow that stuff away."

He shrugged, not *no* but *I guess*, paying more attention to what he was doing than to what I was saying until, head cocked, "Is that your ride?" he said, and I saw headlights in the driveway, Audrey's car. Shrugging into my coat, reaching for my sack of unused supplies and "I'll start the paper tonight," I said, tapping the board; already he had most of it done. "See you tomorrow."

A mild smile, a smile like his tree was a tree. "Sure. See you."

Outside in the driveway, from the car's front seat, I could

still see him, haloed by the kitchen light, alone and working in the quiet house, like a monk. "Did you have a nice time?" Audrey asked, like I was five years old at a play date, *a nice time* but "Yeah," I said, because in a weird kind of way it was true. "Yeah, I did."

Three

Memory, I think, is like a drawing. Sometimes it's a blur, the shadow of a shadow, one form blending and fading into the next until no matter how you try you can't see the picture whole, you can't tell what really happened from what you think you saw. But sometimes it's as plain and clean and straightforward as a blueprint: *this happened, and then this, and then this.* So clear you can see it with your eyes closed. So clear you can't close your eyes.

If I hadn't gotten him into that class . . . so was it all my doing? Was it my karma? Or was it his karma, and I was just along for the ride?

———

Lunchtime Monday, and the empty art room, Snell up on a stepladder staple-gunning a mobile to the ceiling, a Calder mobile, I recognized it from one of my art books. Slim then bulbous, the restless moving shapes and "He's an artist," said Snell, "this friend of yours? He's got the goods?"

Friend of yours? No, not really, one visit to someone's house doesn't mean anything, but "He's a real artist," I said, from underneath the ladder. "You should see his sketchbook, it's better than any portfolio in this class. Even Caitlin Driver's," which was high praise. Caitlin is pretty much the best artist in school (except for McManus, ha ha), *was* the best, because Snell must have gone to see the counselor, and on Wednesday here came Jinsen: into the art room, late slip in hand while the rest of us got out our scrolls, the calligraphy brushes and watercolor trays. Megan rolled her eyes when she saw him walk in but then "What are you *doing*?" to me with real alarm. "You're—He's not going to *sit* with us, is he?"

I won't lie, I felt kind of weird doing it, but then again the whole thing was my idea in the first place, and anyway where else was he going to sit? with McManus? "Calm down," I said to Megan, and made a space for him at our table.

It was almost funny, how she refused to calm down, how she sat with her chair at an angle so she wouldn't accidentally make eye contact with him, or catch his cooties or something, almost funny if it wasn't so incredibly stupid. And Megan's not a stupid person, that's the worst part. . . . But if any of it bothered Jinsen he didn't act like it, just worked on his scroll, the brush like part of his hand, a natural extension and "Do you know what these mean?" I asked him, tapping the translation sheet. "Or are you just going for looks?"

He gave me a little smile; he didn't answer.

When the bell went Jinsen was still cleaning up, Snell heading over to the table but "Come *on*, Justin," from Megan frowning by the door, keeping that frown all the way to the lockers, the parking lot, idling her mom's new red Jeep and "Use the gas pedal, Meg," said Jakob in the back. "We could walk there faster."

And there he was again, no coat, naturally, but the day was halfway warm, it wouldn't have been so bad if someone hadn't thrown a slush-ball at him. I saw him tense right as it hit, imagined the cold slide of slush down his neck and *Let's give him a ride*, I almost said, but I knew Megan never would, especially not today. So instead, as we were sucking down our coffees in the too-warm crush of Cuppa Jane's—

"Cappuccinos," Megan said.

"Cappuccini?" Jakob asked.

—I told them why I'd put Snell onto him, about how cool

his sketchbook was, *Jinsen's a really good artist* but "Ginseng?" Jakob said, raising his eyebrows; he wears those half-moon glasses, he gets a lot into a look. "Is that his name?"

Megan laughed.

"It's *Jinsen*," more sharply than I'd meant. "It's a—spiritual name."

"Really?" said Megan. "Like a religious thing?"

"I think it's Buddhist," I said.

"Really? Like the Dalai Lama and all that?" Head down over her drink, mouth curved in a thoughtful frown. "Listen," she said, gazing up at us, and I thought she was going to say—I don't know, something intelligent, about Buddhism or tolerance or something, but "Listen, did you *hear* what Lauren Tibbets did? LaRonda and those guys will *never* talk to her again."

———

Tapping it with her killer nails, today they were burgundy red and "This is a quite a project," Keller said to me and Jinsen. " 'King Consumer,' very creative."

Well, the *board* was creative; my paper was just OK. But still, put together they netted a big red A—although not for "Tim Elder," Keller said. "I don't see your name here. Weren't you assigned to this group?"

He shrugged but didn't answer, shot me a dirty look, a worse one for Jinsen who'd gone back to his seat, sketchbook out and *Well, that's that*, I thought, *the project's done, I don't have to talk to him again* and shouldn't I be happy? But I didn't feel especially happy. And was I allowed—supposed—to exile him now, from our table in Art? *Go sit in the corner, Buddha Boy.* Preserve a precious feeb-free landscape for Megan and me.

Why was I thinking about all this? What difference did it make to me?

Keller finished handing back the projects, then clicked off the lights for a video on the World Bank, oh joy. Before I settled myself in proper doze position—head propped on fist, leg wedged under desk to keep me upright—I saw Jinsen open his sketchbook, and I wondered before I closed my eyes, *How can he draw in the dark?*

—

They hung like leaves, or curling locks of hair, all the scroll paintings staple-gunned around the art room, fluttering gently, minutely, as everybody walked around looking, pointing, *That one's mine* or *Check that one out*. I didn't like mine much when I saw it: what had felt loose and tumbling, almost abstract in the doing, had come out stiff and straight, as if I'd copied it stroke by stroke from the examples; it was about as creative as a billboard or "An ad," I said to Megan, "for Chinese noodles. A stupid ad—"

"No, *Japanese* noodles, right?—Wow, is that one Caitlin's? *That* one is *good*."

I'd already seen Caitlin's, hanging right by the door: it *was* good, really good, but since this one was great I knew whose it was and I had to smile, smile at him hanging back by our table, orange happy-face T-shirt down to his knees and "Look," someone else said, LaRonda, "look at this one," until most of the class was gathered around it, turning it back and forth to see the name and "All of you," Snell said from the front of the room, "you've all done some really nice stuff. But one person's work is truly outstanding. Take a bow, Michael Martin," as people started looking around, *Michael who?* but as soon as they realized it was Jinsen he was talking about, the dreaded Buddha Boy, they started whispering, a little hissing undercurrent as Snell crossed the room to his scroll and "I'd like to show this to Ed Keeley," Snell said. "At CAC."

And then they really whispered. The Creative Arts Center, it's like a satellite school to Rucher, Advanced Placement art-major types, to be even considered for it as a sophomore was a really big deal. Even Caitlin Driver wasn't going to CAC.

But Jinsen didn't seem to know that; he just smiled a little, and shrugged, the shrug that means *Sure, OK*. But not like he was acting cool, or trying to pretend it didn't matter; just like he was—glad, I guess. Like he was glad that people liked the scroll for itself, whether they liked him or not, but *How can he really be that way?* I thought. Was that the, the religion thing? like the Golden Rule, or Zen, or something? The sound of one hand clapping, right.

And as people shuffled back to their tables, a few kids glanced at Jinsen, little covert glances like *Hmm*. Not that they liked him now or anything, just that he'd surprised them, got their attention in a different way. And some other kids scowled, like he was getting away with something, like Buddha Boy shouldn't be allowed to even think about CAC.

McManus didn't scowl, he didn't even look at Jinsen, but as he turned for his table he deliberately passed by Jinsen's scroll, to flick it, hard, with his knuckles, hard enough to leave a deep dent, like a scar, a shadow I could see from where I sat: between Jinsen and Megan, who had her chair now turned completely backwards, as if she belonged to the table behind us, LaRonda's table. "Grow up," I muttered in her ear, and scooted my own chair away.

And after class, as Megan made a point of leaving without me, I went up to Snell at his desk and "You know," I said, arms crossed, "his name's not Michael."

"Excuse me?"

"Michael Martin, you said. His name is Jinsen."

Locker sounds, bang and holler, someone laughing outside in the hall and "I didn't know that," Snell said; he made a little scribble in his class book. "Thanks for telling me."

By the time I got out to the parking lot, Jakob's gray minivan was gone—*Oh great, thanks a lot, Megan*—so I merged with the sidewalk rush, mush of melted snow showing pocked and dirty, little knots of people talking and huddling, joking around as I detoured past them, head down, pissed off at Megan and McManus and myself—

—and "Don't!" from someone, not loud but urgent. I looked up, just in time to see a scuffle on the steps, then something flying over the crowd—a book? no, a notebook, *thwack* and splash as it hit the muck puddled by the curb, and there was Magnur, laughing, by the doors, laughing at Jinsen who trotted down to fish in the dark slush for his notebook—

—no, not his notebook, his *sketchbook*—

—and then Magnur was shouldering down the steps, Magnur and McManus, who passed right in front of me, who saw me looking and "It's a watercolor now," McManus said, and laughed. "Right, Justin?"

34

I wanted to—to *do* something, say something—*You shit-head, you evil creep*—but I didn't, I just stood there, my mouth glued shut and then they were gone, hopping into someone's car, revving away in a flume of water—

—and there was Jinsen, looking right at me, the ruined book limp and bleeding water through his muddy hands.

Four

"*Justin*," Audrey's voice through my door, the voice she uses when she's called me more than once. "Telephone."

On my bed and staring at the ceiling, at the ancient water stains my dad had never fixed but instead had let me color, lying on my back on a plywood board propped on ladders, *just like Michelangelo*, how old was I then? Seven? Six? "Tell them," I said, pillow over my head, "that I'm not here. Tell them I died."

"It's your father."

Door cracked, my hand out and then "Hey, Justin," a metal echo in my ear, like he was shouting from inside a tin can, a tin can stranded in a wind tunnel. "God, what a lousy connection—want me to call back?"

The pillow was still over my head, holding the phone in place. "No," I said. "I can hear you."

We hadn't talked in a while, but he didn't ask how I was, or how school was, or if I had any girlfriends, none of the usual lame divorced-dad stuff other people say they have to put up with. Mostly he just told me what was happening with him: a painting he was working on, a gallery that might be interested in showing his work, how he'd fixed the fan belt on his car—but all the while his voice was like a hand holding mine, warm and strong, the more he talked the more I relaxed, the pillow retreated until "I was thinking," he said, "about you coming out here for spring break. What do you think?"

"I don't know. Maybe."

"You know, you don't sound so hot. Something wrong?"

Audrey would have said *Something's wrong* like she already knew what it was whether she did or not. Which is why I could always talk to my dad, why I could tell him, now, about Jinsen, about "King Consumer" and the scroll painting: "Snell wants some guy from CAC to look at it," I said; my dad knew what that meant, he used to teach part-time at CAC. "You'd like it, I know you would. You'd like all his stuff—"

"I'd like to see it. This kid's a buddy of yours?"

37

My silence; and the tin can–wind tunnel sound, the distance rushing between us but he didn't try to cover that distance, that silence, he didn't say anything, he just waited until "He's—strange," I said, muffled again by the pillow. "He begs at lunch, he shaves his head. . . . No one likes him."

Silence.

"But he's a really good artist."

Silence: the waiting kind, waiting for what? and then suddenly out it came, a dark rushed jumble of sketchbook and McManus and Jinsen at the curb and "I didn't *say* anything," I said now, crushing the pillow harder against the side of my head. "I just stood there like a, like—And when Megan and Jakob pulled up I just—I left him," alone on the sidewalk, sketchbook wet against his chest, as I jumped into the minivan, into an instant argument with Megan, yelling at her while she yelled at me until Jakob yelled at us both and "What was I supposed to do?" I said, to my dad, to myself, to Jinsen at the curb. "It was too late anyway, the book was already ruined."

He didn't say anything: not like he disagreed, or was mad at me—I don't think my dad has ever been mad at me—but like it was my problem and what was I going to do about it? And I didn't know, I didn't say anything, just listened to the

38

tin-can sounds, and wished that my dad were here, in the house, right now. Finally, in his gentlest voice, "Let me know," he said, "about spring break, all right? And now let me talk to your mother."

———

So what *was* I supposed to do? now, today, when I'd spent the whole lunch hour avoiding the cafeteria so I wouldn't have to see him, squeaked in tardy to Econ so I wouldn't have to talk—although I wanted to say something, even if it was late and lame and useless, *McManus is a bastard, don't let it get you down.* . . . But the thing was, he didn't *look* down, he didn't look sad or mad or like anything but himself, sitting there kitty-corner with his backpack at his feet like a big dumb dog no one had ever trained, sprawling into the aisle between us as "Open to Chapter Nine," Keller said, and we did, he did, book propped on its end like a privacy fence, reaching into his backpack for his sketchbook, the same one? Yes: see the scuffed-up cover, pages wavy from wet, I could hardly stand to look at it, how could he bear to use it anymore?

"The Federal Reserve," Keller said, holding up one finger, "serves what function in our economy?"

Maybe he couldn't afford another one? But no, remember that tackle box full of art supplies? so maybe he wanted this one, wanted to keep it, why would anyone want that? and "You want to see?" in a murmur, he wasn't looking at me but somehow he knew I was looking; how? But no matter what, mess, ruin, disaster, I did want to see, I put out my hand, he passed me the book—

"—our nation's money supply. Now, if the Fed wants to lower prices—"

—open to a landscape, delicate trees around a gray irregular pond, some tiny creatures in the foreground, drinking, as small as it was the detail was amazing. And he'd done it in a kind of wash, like figures glimpsed through mist, some parts obscured and others sharp, almost hyper-real: the way the animals' legs bent, the irregular shape of the pond, not just a neat little oval but the way it would really look—

—but how had he done it? when the paper itself was ruined, a spoiled landscape, how did—

—and then, still looking, all of a sudden I *saw*: that the pond was a blotch from muddy water, silty and dark, the mist was where he'd tried to sponge it away . . . but he hadn't been able to clean it so he'd, what, he'd *used* it, used the dirt left behind—

—and I started flipping back and forth, looking and seeing: woolly sheep clustered on a hill, a storm coming in from the sea, a little town under a skyful of clouds and all of them, all the drawings I saw, were built on the damage and the stains, one page had mud thick enough to scratch with your finger but he'd made the mud into a mountain range, impersonal and brooding, he'd made something meant to be ugly into something more than beautiful, something real—

—and I smiled, a bright hot smile, a smile like, what's the word? *vindication*, like Oh take *that*, McManus, you bastard, take it and stick it up your big red—

"—twelve districts, each with its own Federal Reserve Bank. . . . Is this information somehow funny to you, Justin?"

"Uh, no," but I couldn't stop smiling, in a minute I'd be laughing out loud so I had to hide in my Econ book, pretend I was taking notes. But the smile's heat stayed alive inside me, and I felt it for the rest of the day.

Five

"—want to split a double-chocolate scone? Justin? Are you zoned out or what?"

Cuppa Jane's at 3:30, extra-stuffy, extra-loud, an extra-long line in which we were stranded way toward the back and "No," I said, shifting my backpack, "no thanks. Too much chocolate."

" 'Too much chocolate'?" rolling her eyes, "there's no such *thing*," but Megan smiled when she said it, all that yelling in the van had kind of cleared the mental air between us where Jinsen was concerned. And even though she still wouldn't talk to him in class, at least she'd stopped turning her chair around.

Jakob hadn't gone on the record either way, for or

against Jinsen; Jakob, I thought, was just watching. Like he watched Lauren Tibbets now, up ahead in the endless line, and "Did you know," he said to us, peering over his glasses, "that Lauren Tibbets's laugh is so high only dogs can hear it?"

"Only dogs would *want* to. Justin, you're coming with us to tryouts, right? For *Fiddler*?" Megan had suddenly decided that we were all trying out for the spring musical, even though none of us could sing, *especially* since none of us could sing, but "I can't," I said, because I was going over to Jinsen's, although I didn't say that and they didn't ask.

Since the sketchbook thing I'd felt—I don't know, not that I owed him anything, and for sure he never acted that way, but it still seemed as if there was something I ought to be doing with him, or maybe for him, I'm not explaining it very well but that was the way I felt. Karma, right? So when Snell came up with this project, for Jinsen to make a welcome banner for a CAC show—something about a dragon, or a lion, and Asian art—and when Jinsen asked would I help him do it, right away I said yes.

So there I was, heading toward his house, half-drawn blinds and rusty minivan, to see in the driveway another car, a too-big car like old ladies like to drive, and here came, yes, an old lady dainty down the steps, tiny and birdy and bent.

But she was way too old for a mom, too ragged, too, must be a housekeeper or something.

As the car pulled away I forgot about her, wondering again where Jinsen's family was, he had to have parents somewhere, didn't he? at least one, to pay the bills?—but then Jinsen showed up, key in the lock, stepping into the ghost of old incense and the silence like a blanket, not covering something up but keeping it in, protecting it the way a blanket covers a baby, or a hand holds a jewel, does that make sense?

Even the dim kitchen felt friendlier this time. Maybe because the space heater was really kicking, filling the room with warmth; maybe because we were talking about art and I was telling him about my dad, what a great painter he was, how he'd work for months just to get one color right. "I've got one of his paintings in my room," I said. "It's abstract, kind of like a circle in red and green. . . . It's really cool, you should see it."

"I'd like to," he said, and I thought, *Did I just invite him over? I guess so.*

As we worked on the preliminary sketch—which means he worked and I watched, throwing in a suggestion here and there—we talked: about the banner, and art class, and school in general, and "What was your old school like?" I said. "Like Rucher, or was it actually human?"

Unspooling the template paper, "It was—" and he stopped. "It wasn't like Rucher. Smaller, a lot smaller. A lot poorer, too."

I could believe that; a lot of schools would seem poor compared to Rucher. "Did you like it there?"

He looked not at me but at the banner; then, dry, "It was OK," which made me wonder if he missed it, if he'd had friends he left behind; good friends, not like me. Maybe it was the kind of school where people were nice to each other, where there were no social rules or cutthroat cliques. If there was such a school.

He kept staring at the banner, as if he were far away, maybe back in his old school, old life, why had he moved here anyway? Maybe his parents changed jobs, or got transferred or something. "Do your parents, like, work all the time? Is that why they're never home?"

Head bent to the paper, carefully erasing, carefully resketching a line and "My parents are dead," he said. What is there to say to that? *I'm sorry*? *Tough break*? I tried to imagine it for myself, my own life: no more Audrey asking questions, no more Dad on the phone . . . it was a dry, lunar feeling, like being stranded a million miles from home. "This is my great-aunt's place," he said. "But she's pretty old, you know, she goes to the doctor a lot. So I'm usually on my own."

"Your great-aunt?" and then I flashed back to the lady on the steps, dandelion hair, big cloudy glasses, *pretty old,* that was her? "We do OK together," Jinsen said, his gaze still on the paper. "It's not so bad."

Not so bad: parents gone, school gone, nothing left but the ancient great-aunt, which meant lots of pills, right, and crappy microwave dinners, and lights out probably at nine o'clock. Then get himself to school in the morning—he must leave really early to walk all that way—and spend the day putting up with McManus and all the rest of the jerks, throwing stuff at him, calling him names. . . . I felt—I didn't know what I felt: not sorry for him, like he was pathetic or something, to live like that he'd have to be pretty damn tough. But the whole thing completely pissed me off, like why should he *have* to live that way? Wasn't it bad enough to be without any family and have to do everything yourself? Why couldn't people just leave him alone?

But I didn't know how to say any of that, I didn't know what to say so I just sat there, watching him work until "Hey," I said, to change the subject. "Does a dragon have a muzzle like that?"

He smiled then, a sideways smile and "It's not supposed to be a dragon," he said. "It's supposed to be a lion. A snow lion. Like in Tibet."

46

"Oh," I said, like I knew. "Sure."

"My father went to Tibet once. He said it was really beautiful there."

My father: I tried to imagine an older Jinsen, bald head and all, like the monks in the pictures: calm-looking men in trailing robes, smiling closed-eyed statues and "Is this all, like, Buddhist stuff?" I asked, pointing to one of the magazines.

"Some of it. Some is Christian," showing me another magazine, a guy with a circle-shaved head like Friar Tuck, and a big silver cross around his neck. "Are you Christian?"

"My dad is, I think. I'm not really anything. I mean, I don't believe in that stuff."

"Yeah?" he said. Then when he'd finished the lion's face he set down his pencil and "Come here," he said. "Take a look at this."

Crossing the hall from the kitchen, leading me into a dark little room that, with the light clicked on, burst completely into color: sky blue and saffron yellow, purest orange, seafoam green, and all of it waving, undulating, each color flowing into the next because the colors were *alive*, were people: a dancing woman with a pointy tongue, a man with an elephant's head, a smiling guy who looked Jesus-y, a Buddha with electric blond hair. There were others I couldn't guess but I could have spent the whole day looking, detail on detail—like there, in that flower, a girl-face, or the gray eyes gazing out of a cloud—and all of it, as you investigated, drawing you deeper and deeper, all four walls one amazing, unending mural.

Past the walls, if you could look past them, the rest of the room was eat-off-the-floor clean: white plastic blinds and a bed like an Army cot, a folded-up exercise mat, and something like a little altar, a bright blue candle and some beads and "All religions," he said, "are about the same thing really, aren't they? I mean they dress differently and use different words, but it's all about the same thing."

Which made zero sense to me. I mean, how could all religions be the same? Like Catholics and Muslims and Jews and all that, they had nothing in common except how wrong each thought all the others were, it was like saying me and Jinsen and, and McManus were all basically the same, it was *crazy* and "That's crazy," I said, louder than I meant to. "That's not how it is at all."

"Why is it crazy?" Head to one side, he was smiling: but not a know-it-all smile, he just looked—happy. "Don't you think God is the same everywhere, no matter what you call Him? or Her? Or Them?"

My gaze was back on the colors, the people, the calm

gray eyes in the cloud and "I don't think about God," I said, waiting for him to say *Maybe you should start* or *He thinks about you* or something religious like that. But he didn't, he just stood there looking at the walls with me, like we were tourists in a gallery until "I guess we should get back to work," he said, and clicked off the bedroom light.

Six

"So I'm one of the villagers, right? wearing this *scarf*, this *babushka*, I look like my own grandmother. Then Kendra gets up to sing, like *'sing'* in quotes—"

"You should have heard her," Jakob said, munching a french fry. "It was atrocious. And then Freeberg is like, Aren't there any real *belters* here? and Meg gets right up front and says—"

" 'I can belt,' " through a mouthful of mocha smoothie. "And I already knew the words, or some of them, anyway. . . . So now I'm playing *Golde*! Isn't that *amazing*?"

"Congratulations," I said; I tried my best to sound excited. "That's really—that's great." I knew they were talking about Mr. Freeberg, the drama teacher, and *Fiddler on the*

Roof, but that was all I knew: I hadn't gone to watch rehearsal. I didn't know who Golde was, I hadn't seen much of Megan and Jakob for the past couple of weeks. I wasn't sure if it had to do with Jinsen, with me helping him make the lion banner, or if it was because of the play, but we three just weren't as close right now. It was like they were on an ice floe, slowly drifting away from me. Or maybe I was the one drifting.

We still ate lunch together, though, like we were doing today: Jakob and Megan on one side of the table, me on the other, sharing an order of fries—but my glance kept going past them, over to Jinsen, sitting quietly in his corner. He wasn't allowed to go around to the tables anymore, Mr. Valente said it was "disruptive," so instead he sat by the end of the hot-lunch line, a yellow plastic bowl—his begging bowl, he called it—in his lap, *in case someone wants to give me something.* Mainly they gave him nothing, except when some smart-ass tossed in a gum wrapper, or Magnur whipped pennies at him, of course you don't see Valente down here calling that disruptive, do you? No, that's just "horseplay." Sometimes one of the cafeteria workers would give him some free food, but mostly he just sat there, day after day.

And day after day I sat watching, feeling more and more

uncomfortable. I'd asked him once if he had to do that, beg, to be a monk, or whatever he was trying to be; and he just smiled, he didn't say yes or no, but I was asking the wrong question, wasn't I? Because the right question was, maybe, What difference did it make if he wanted to beg? Or: Who was he hurting? Or: Why couldn't they just leave him alone? as "Ready?" from Megan, rising, tray in hand. "You *have* to see the guy who plays the Fiddler, Justin, he's *such* a major—"

"Justin?" Jakob peering over his glasses. "You coming?"

"In a minute," I said, and I started walking, hand in my pocket, through the cafeteria that seemed bigger as I crossed it, bigger and louder and more full of people, walking all the way to where Jinsen sat with his bowl.

"Hi," he said; black T-shirt and gleaming head, egg-smooth, he must have just shaved it again and "Hi," I said, and put the rest of my week's lunch money in his bowl, folded bills and a couple of quarters, just put it there and turned around and "Hey, Justin," from someone behind me: Hooks, one of McManus's boys, standing there smirking and "How come you're givin' him money, man?" Through a big wet mouthful of chips. "Is he, like, your buddy or something?" "Chew with your mouth shut," I said, and pushed past him, out the doors and into the hall where Megan and

Jakob were nowhere, where people spilled past and around me, where the bloodred banner on the wall showed a pair of roaring black lions, RUCHER CAN'T <u>SUCCEED</u> WITHOUT <u>U</u>!

Later, in the too-hot car with Audrey—a dentist appointment, I left at fifth hour—I sat with my head against the window, the cool glass kind to my skin. "How come we never go to church?" I said.

"What?" I could feel her look without having to see it, wide-eyed and startled; she turned the radio down. "What did you say?"

"I said, why don't we ever go to church? Why didn't you ever take me when I was little?"

"Why are—what brought this on?" Half bewildered mom, half district attorney. "Did someone—"

"I just asked," I said, and closed my eyes; she kept talking but I didn't listen, focusing instead on the radio jazz, its silvery, whispering horns until "Justin," sharp, "I'm talking to you. Did someone ask you about this? One of your teachers, or—"

"No one asked me anything." *I mean, I don't believe in that stuff.* The kind of stuff that makes you sit around in cafeterias, letting people throw pennies at you; the kind of stuff that keeps you there when a normal person, a person like me, say, would just give up, give in, go away. "I just—wanted to know."

"I see," she said.

That night my dad called; Audrey had asked him to, I knew, she always calls him when something happens with me that she doesn't understand. Half-asleep over Language Arts homework, phone to my ear, and "Hey," my dad said; he doesn't waste time. "What's all this talk about religion?"

"Nothing," I said; I shut my bedroom door. "I just asked her about church, and stuff. . . . You still go?"

"Sure."

"To that same place we went? With the, the organ and the windows and all that?"

"Not that place. But one just like it."

"Have you ever been to a, a Buddhist church? A temple?"

He paused, then "No, actually I haven't. Why? You want to go to one?"

My turn to pause: *No. Yes. I don't know.* "Maybe. Just to see what it's like."

If it was Audrey she would have asked why, she would have kept going until she found out, but "Sure," he said. "We can do that."

I thought about Jinsen in the cafeteria, I thought about the mural in his room and "Dad" I asked, my voice sounding strained, even to me, "what do you know about Buddhism?"

"Not a lot, frankly. There's the bodhi tree, and the Four Noble Truths—"

"But do you think all that's—right? Religion, I mean? Do you think it's the right thing to do?"

He didn't answer at first; I could hear the distance again, not a tin can this time but a sound like the ocean, slow waves of silence and night, past midnight where he was, and then finally "A lot of bad things," he said, "have been done in God's name. And most of the greatest good, too. It's like I keep telling you, kiddo—use your eyes."

———

I heard about it before I saw it, from John Kindel in Algebra, *It was in the bathroom, man*: stuck like trash in a urinal, wet and filthy and spoiled and "If I find out who's responsible," said Snell—standing arms crossed at the front of the room, his voice shaking, he was so mad—"*when* I find out, that person is going to be in trouble. And if you," his hard gaze like a laser, moving one by one around the Art room, "if *any* of you know who did this, know and don't tell, then you're just as guilty as that person. And just as cruel."

No one said anything; the room was so quiet you could

hear someone laughing in the computer lab next door. On the walls hung the untouched scrolls, calm as leaves on a tree. But someone had ripped down Jinsen's scroll, ripped it down and stuffed it in the toilet. A few of the others were gone, too, LaRonda's, I think, and Laine Hanson's—and Josh Winston's, which was how I knew, *knew* it was McManus, he couldn't bear to wreck his own work even to throw off suspicion but he didn't mind doing it to Winston, who was such a henchman, such a kiss-ass, he wouldn't even care. . . . Look at the two of them, glancing around all silent and serious like they were trying to figure out who did it, looking at everyone but Jinsen who sat, face empty, backpack on his lap, like a refugee driven out of his homeland, trying to think where to go next.

"We were going to start a new project today," Snell said. Now he sounded tired, almost as tired as Jinsen looked. "But to be honest, until I know who did this, I don't feel like working with any of you. So treat this like a seminar hour. Do your homework, or silent reading, or something. Just keep it quiet," and he went back to his desk and sat there, not even pretending to work, as people started opening their backpacks, taking out notebooks, everyone but Jinsen, who just kept sitting there, and me, who sat looking at nothing, at my hands clenched on my knees because I was afraid if I moved an inch I would hit something, or start yelling, I didn't know what I would do.

Megan whispered to me, whispered my name; I ignored her. The only one I could have talked to then was Jinsen, but I didn't, I didn't do anything for the whole hour, I just sat there until the bell rang and everyone moved as one, relieved, released, into the hall where at once the buzz started, *do you* and *I think* and "It was Colonel Mustard," Josh Winston said, mock-serious. "In the lavatory, with the scroll."

And McManus smiled, just that, just a modest little smile and when I saw it I felt hot all over, I felt like I had that day at the curb, choked and silent and I wanted to punch him, I wanted to kill him, I had to do something—

—so I went back into the Art room, up to Snell at his desk, my mouth was open but I had no proof, *no proof* other than I knew it was true, knew it was him, and "Mr. Snell," I said, and he took one look at me and said, flat, "Shut the door."

———

"Will you do it over?"

The clicking tick of the space heater; the burnt-apple incense smell. Jinsen still seemed tired, but he looked better than I felt, which was sick to my stomach, a sour taste lodged in my throat despite about a gallon of Coke and "No," he said, pausing in his drawing to put a new lead in the mechanical pencil. "I couldn't, really, even if I wanted to. But I don't want to. What would be the point?"

"The point," harsh, "would be the same thing you did with the sketchbook. The *point* would be to show that shithead that he can't stop you, that he—what?" because he was shaking his head, slow, almost sad and "Come on, Justin," he said. The overhead light washed shadows down his cheeks, making him look older, like a real monk, someone stern and wise and "That's not why I saved my sketchbook," he said. "You of all people should know that."

I didn't say anything; I didn't know that. I hadn't even known how to say what I had to say to Snell, I'd just stood there like a chunk of wood, dumb stick with my mouth open, and even when the door was shut I couldn't speak, I didn't have the words so he had to say *You know who did this, Justin?* All I could do was shrug, hands out, like yes and no until finally *You think you know?* and then I could speak, not straight out but at an angle: *McManus knows* and Snell nodded, looking past me at the scrolls, maybe McManus's, its stiff little curlicues and whorls.

We'll keep this between us, Snell said. *Thanks for coming in.*

And back in the hall I looked straight ahead, I didn't see McManus or his goon squad, I didn't see Megan or Jakob, I didn't talk to anyone until I got to Jinsen's house, a long cold walk and a longer wait, my butt and legs were almost totally numb by the time he got there but by then the numbness inside had worn off and I was *pissed*, for the first ten minutes all I did was yell; Jinsen never yelled. He just turned on the space heater, got out his supplies, unrolled the banner—we were past the sketch stage now, we were—he was—working on the real thing, on cream-colored paper heavy as cloth—and started to draw.

And now "Come on," he said again, and tapped his pencil on the table: two taps, *tick-tick,* like a teacher would do. "Why would I want to use my drawing like a, a stick, to hit somebody, to hurt them? Why would you think that's the right thing to do?"

The murmur of the space heater; the early dark outside. I didn't answer.

"Would your dad do that with his painting?"

"Shit! Aren't you even *pissed*?" Loud and hard, an alien voice, but I was mad, and even madder that he wasn't. "Don't you even want to kick his ass, or get even, or *anything*?"

"Look," hands flat on the table, bald head pale as a

moon, "I'm not *happy* about this, all right? I worked really hard on that scroll, I was going to—" And he sighed, a hard sound, a sound forced out by pressure but "Don't you see," he said, "if I tried to get even I'd be worse than he is, I'd be more *wrong* than he is. Because he doesn't know. But I do."

"Know what?"

"That we're all gods," he said. "Gods inside, all of us. Him too."

Incense like smoke from a fire, his stare on me like a searchlight, a light that knows your name, and I thought of the mural, the blond Buddha and the smiling Jesus guy, the swirl of colors like moving living things and "Gods," I said, "oh that's just *great*. Well, guess what? You're right, McManus *is* a god, he's the god of the assholes, he's the god of that school, and if you don't do something he's going to keep on, he's going to keep after you until you *have* to do something whether you want to or not!" On my feet now, yelling down at him. "And I don't want to sit here and watch it!"

He didn't say anything, just looked up at me, not mad at me either, and "Fine," I said, "just forget the whole thing." Grabbing my jacket, storming out into that darkness slick now with silver sleet, I almost fell about a hundred times, in fact I did fall coming up my own driveway, hard on my knees in the wet and the ice, I had to grab onto Audrey's bumper to keep from landing on my face.

And on the porch, the door swung wide and "*There* you are," she said: coat on, keys in hand, she was mad but I was madder and "Where were you, Justin? I—"

"Leave me alone," I said, and pushed past her, down the hall and into my room, where I slammed the door so hard my dad's painting shivered on the wall, where I flung myself on my bed in the dark, breathing in and out, in and out, sour taste and incense echo, the cold ammonia smell of my own sweat.

Seven

In history, in a movie, in a book, you can always tell who the heroes are: they're the ones rushing into the burning building, giving crucial testimony in the courtroom, refusing to step to the back of the bus. They're the ones who act the way you hope you would, if the moment came to you.

But the movies and the history books never tell you how they felt, those heroes, if they were angry or uncertain or afraid, if they had to think a long time before they did the right thing, if they even knew what the right thing was or just made a headlong guess, just leaped and hoped they landed instead of falling. They never tell you what it's like to stand on the brink, wishing you were somewhere—or someone—else, wishing the choice had never come your way and you could just go back to your safe, ordinary, everyday life.

Because you know what else the books never say? Nobody, hero or not, really wants to rush into a fire. Because fire burns.

———

"But *Tevye*—"

Onstage, in the crowd scene, someone snickered; Megan, up front, kept her face politely straight and "It's pronounced 'Tev-ee-uh,' not 'TV,' " said Mr. Freeberg. He was a little guy, with flaring black hair and a Harvard sweatshirt; he could have been one of the actors. "Try it again."

"But *Tevye*—"

"She's a cheerleader," Jakob murmured to me, "can't you tell? . . . You know, most of these people can't act. It's really kind of painful to watch."

"Then why are you here?"

"Why are *you* here?" which was a very good question: why *was* I there, at this lunch-hour rehearsal, squashed knees-up in the auditorium's back row, choking down one of Jakob's awful FuBars ("Tofu on the Go!"). Why wasn't I in the cafeteria eating real food? or watching out for Jinsen, who was probably under siege in his corner, getting it good from McManus after all that stuff in Art?

But who made Jinsen my problem, anyway? Jinsen was Jinsen's problem, with his bald head and his begging bowl and his everyone's-a-god stuff, *gods inside*, yeah *right*. What kind of a person could actually believe that? That didn't have anything to do with religion, regular go-to-church religion. That was just crazy.

And anyway he'd never actually asked me to do anything, had he? to look out for him or be his friend or anything like that? We'd worked on the banner together but the real truth was he had talent enough to make fifty banners blindfolded, all I was good for was sharpening his pencils but he had mechanical pencils so he didn't even need me for *that*, did he? The fact was, he didn't need me at all.

Which was what I'd told myself all night, lying wide-eyed and angry as the red digital minutes ticked by, one o'clock, three o'clock, quarter to five, what I'd argued myself into until it wasn't even arguing anymore, just agreeing, just relief . . . so I fell asleep for two whole hours, a sleep like a locked door without any dreams at all, a sleep I woke from determined to do nothing because there was nothing I had to do, was there? I'd already done the right thing, I'd told Snell what had happened, and now it was his problem, and Jinsen's, and McManus's if they ever proved anything which of course they wouldn't, so life would go on as it always had and I was out of the whole mess, for now and forever and for good.

So why was I hunched in the back row like a fugitive, eating this tasteless lump of "food" that would gag a cockroach, watching Megan pretend she was a nineteenth-century Jewish lady named Golde with five daughters, two of whom were at least a foot taller than she was? Why wasn't I in the cafeteria, going on with my own life? Why was I still worried about Jinsen, who didn't even have enough brains to be worried about himself?

"You're supposed to be upset," Freeberg told the cheer-leader; he sounded kind of upset himself. "You're not supposed to smile when you say it. . . . Try it again."

"But *Tevye*—"

Jakob rolled his eyes at me. "Isn't it tragic?" he muttered. *Gods inside*; the scroll in the toilet; *thanks for coming in.* When you've already done the right damn thing, why should you have to keep on doing it? and "It sure is," I said, handing him back his FuBar. "I gotta go."

———

In the hall, digging in my locker, a minute or two before the bell and "Hey," from right behind me: McManus, hands in his pockets, head cocked to one side. "Hey, Justin."

Lots of people, passing by; but no one saw, no one

stopped. The rest of the crew—Magnur, Hooks, Winston—stood a few paces back, like dogs on a leash, a pack of dogs. Waiting.

McManus stepped closer, closing in on me. "You're not spreading any rumors," he said, "are you? Because I've been hearing some. About me. So if you have anything you want to say to me, you better say it right now."

I could hear the blood in my ears, my heartbeat, rising; I stood silent in that sound, wondering what they were going to do, if they were going to do it now or wait for later. Finally, when I didn't—wouldn't—speak, McManus said, "I hear you're hanging out with that freak Buddha Boy. I don't think that's such a good idea either."

My own voice then, low and dry, as if it came from someone else: "You hear a lot of things, don't you."

And he reached out, fast, so fast past me to slam my locker door, slam it with all his force, if I hadn't jumped it would have caught my fingers, crushed my fingers and "I hear everything," he said, and walked away.

Eight

A surprise, Audrey had said, but she wouldn't tell me what it was, just *Make sure you're home by six o'clock,* so I left Jinsen's early, and surly, to find some strange Jeep in the driveway, a glossy black hulk with tires five feet tall, *who's that?—*

—and there he was in the living room, baseball cap and five o'clock shadow, he laughed when he saw the look on my face. "You hungry?" my dad said. "I am."

"It's a school night," said Audrey. "Try not to be too late," but she was smiling, too, at me, at both of us, at all of us; for just that one minute, we were all together again.

Outside I had to jump to get into the Jeep, brand-new rental with power everything, half the stuff my dad couldn't even figure out how to use. "The thing's more complicated than a jet fighter," he said; he thought it was hilarious. "Plus it handles like a tank in this slush, who would even want a car like this?"

"Everyone at my school," I said.

"I asked for something *sturdy*, but. . . . You want Italian for dinner? or Thai? Your mother says there's a good Thai place on Route 9. Or we could go to Maria's," looking down at a scrap of directions, Audrey's crisp firm handwriting, so we went to Maria's, waxy wine bottles and checkered tablecloths, fake ferns in golden pots. "How long are you here for?" I said, sipping my Coke.

"Just tonight. I'm due in the morning," upstate at a gallery, curating a show of someone's paintings, some friend of his, I didn't really get what it was all about but I didn't really care: I was just glad to see him, to listen to him talk, to pretend to myself that we could do this anytime we wanted, go out to dinner on a dreary Tuesday night, escape from the real world and "To be honest," he said, "I'm not totally crazy about his paintings. They're too representational, they're—But when he told me the gallery was in Northfield, I jumped." And he smiled, and I smiled, because I knew he meant *I jumped at the chance to see you.*

The waitress brought our order, my spaghetti and his sloppy salad, antipasto olives and cheese. "Have you thought at all," he said, as I cracked a breadstick, "about spring break? Coming out to visit, I mean?"

"Yeah," I said. Spring break, a million years from now. "I'd like to."

"Will you be done with your project by then? You and the artist?"

The artist: that's what my dad would call him, not the monk, the leper, *that freak Buddha Boy* who was more isolated than ever, now, more than ever a moving target: because Snell had punished McManus, exiled him from our hour to third-hour wasteland, lots of lowly freshmen and none of his buddies, so of course he was taking it out on Jinsen every way he could.

It was sickening, and stupid, so stupid the things they did. Not just throwing pennies or jamming his locker or squirting him with ketchup—though they did all that too—but even uglier stuff, like spitting on his seat in class, or trying to trip him going down the stairs, or body-checking him in the hallways, shoving him into the lockers. . . . But it was never McManus actually doing it, of course, it was Josh Winston and Hooks and Magnur, and even the lesser satellites, the wannabes who were happy to shine with McManus if all they had to do was be mean to the school outcast who was a freak anyway, so it wasn't as bad as picking on a real person, it was like he somehow deserved it, right?

And Jinsen acting as if he agreed with them, just taking everything they threw, sucking it up, sometimes he even laughed at what they did, and that was the worst of all: because it made them even madder, like they weren't hurting him *enough* so they'd have to try even harder, keep trying till they got it right. *Right?*

"—wrong?" Leaning forward to look at me, a dark steady gaze that reminded me of Jinsen's. "Justin. Are you OK?"

Am I OK? Sure. It's not me they're doing it to, it's not me who has to run that gauntlet every day. I'm just the guy who sneaks over in the afternoons to watch him work, see the growing beauty of the banner, it was amazing, what he was doing, the lion was coming to life and "He uses all these colors that don't go together," I said. "But somehow they do."

The waitress came back, more breadsticks, another tiny dish of garlic butter and "Is everything all right?" she asked, looking at my messed-up plate: stain of greasy red sauce, hard little breadstick shards. "Is there something wrong with your meal?"

"No," I said, face stretched into a counterfeit smile. "No, it's fine."

When she turned away my dad sighed, a wind-tunnel sound, set down his glass and "I hear," he said, "that you've really befriended this kid."

70

"Hear from who?"

"Your mother."

Befriended, sure. Without me he'd've never had so much free ketchup—and pennies, don't forget the pennies. "We just hang out," I said. "At his, his great-aunt's house. . . . His parents are dead. Both of them." I stabbed my fork at the limp, wet spaghetti, swirled it, let it drop. All the joy had gone out of the night, the sense of freedom, of escape, my dad seemed to feel it too because "You want to get going?" and he signaled for the waitress, check please, and did I want a doggy bag? No thanks.

Out on the highway the slush had frozen, slippery chunks and sheets of ice, my dad's grip tight on the wheel: "No traction," he said, to me, to himself, to the Jeep whose interior lights glowed a fuzzy yellow-green, the same color Jinsen was using for the lion's eyes: *Like new leaves*, dipping the brush. *New trees in the spring* and "Dad?" I said, before knowing I would say it. "Can I bring him with me? For spring break?"

Headlights, streetlights flickering past, I could feel the shudder of the road, treacherous, unsteady, but "Your friend the artist?" he said, mild. "Sure, why not? He can show me those colors that don't go together."

Spring break, a million years, five and a half weeks away and "OK," I said, "OK, thanks," and sank back against the seat, thinking of the studio, its quiet and its light, thinking, *Maybe Dad can talk to him, make him see, use your eyes* and "Thanks," I said again when we pulled into the driveway. "You'll like him, I know."

"Any friend of yours," he said, and reached over to squeeze my forearm, just once, just lightly, just enough.

The porch light shone on the wet front steps, Audrey's fifty-thousand-watt burglar beacon. I looked at it, not my dad, wanting him to come into the house, wanting him not to go, wanting to go with him. "Are you—can you stay here tonight?"

The quiet throb of the engine, his hands back on the wheel and "I can't, kiddo," he said. "But I'm glad I came. . . . See you in a month and some, right?"

"Right," and then I was out of the Jeep, out in the cold, into the warm house where Audrey was pretending not to be waiting for me, she waved at the window as the headlights retreated and grew small. "Did you go to that Thai place?" she asked as I passed. "It's nice, isn't it?"

"We went to Maria's," I said, and closed my bedroom door.

Nine

"I didn't know," said Megan, sighting down her straw, "that Dead Poets were *allowed* to wear Sparkle Kitty shirts." Nodding at Sara Thackery, member in good standing in what people called the Dead Poets' Society, the ones who wear black lipstick, black everything, hang out smoking at lunchtime and never smile. "Although hers *is* dyed kind of purple. Kind of purplish-black."

"Maybe she's making a statement," Jakob said, carefully unwrapping his FuBar. " 'Sparkle Kitty is for Everyone!' or something. What do you think, Justin?"

"I think it's nobody's damn business what she wears."

Silence: I wasn't looking but I could feel them look, first at each other, then at me and "Justin," Megan said, in a different voice; she put aside her candy bar, a Nutty Goody!, her idea of a balanced lunch. "When are you going to talk to Mr. Smell?"

Talking to Snell was Megan's idea, or her second idea; her first was me going to the peer mediator, the person who's supposed to help when you have a problem with someone in school: peer mediator, counselor, Dean of Students, that's the chain. But our peer mediator was Brian Frame, a big St. Bernard football jocko who was friends with Magnur, so he was out of the question. Plus, I once saw him throw a soda can at Jinsen.

So *Talk to Mr. Smell*, Megan had said, urged, nagged me for a week, but what else could he do? He'd already kicked McManus out of our hour. Besides, look what happened the last time I talked to him.

Still, "You have to *do* something," Megan said. "LaRonda said she heard—God, I *hate* McAnus."

"Heard what?"

Silence.

"Heard *what*?" as Jakob frowned over his tofu, Megan picked at her nails, she always picks her nails when she's nervous and "Just that, that McAnus is—mad at you. Because he thinks you told about the scroll."

"Everyone," I said, "knows he did it. Anyone could have told."

74

"I know, but because of Budd—because of Jinsen," carefully, "he *really* thinks it's you. Because you guys are friends. . . . *Please*, Justin, please just talk to Mr. Smell."

So after school, waiting for the art room to clear, for the hall to quiet down and "What's up, Justin?" Mr. Snell at his desk, sorting through a pile of brushes, big ones, small ones, smooth or bent. "You need a form?"

"A form?"

Eyebrows raised, backwards-tapping the poster on the corkboard, EXPRESS YOURSELF! in the student art competition, *forms due on Friday* and "Your scroll painting was pretty good, I thought. Or you might want to enter something new."

"No, I—" Voices outside, and I waited, listening, thinking all at once of the resistance guys we were doing in History, the underground fighters in World War II, *ordinary citizens doing extraordinary things,* but I wasn't very extraordinary, was I? No, *ordinary* was the word for me, just an ordinary coward, afraid of getting caught in an empty stairway, or surrounded in the gym, afraid of the way McManus had smiled when he slammed my locker door, *he thinks you told about the scroll,* but that was wrong because he *knew* I'd told, the same way I knew that he'd done it and "Mr. Snell," I said; my voice sounded dry. "Can I shut the door?"

But shut door or not, sympathetic or not—and he *was*

sympathetic, I could tell by the way he talked, by what he said and didn't say—still he wasn't much help: "I've already changed Mark's hour, and I've talked the whole thing over with Mr. Koss," the vice-principal, wrestler's arms and chain-smoker's hack, we called him The Terminator. "But unless Jinsen himself makes some kind of complaint, there's really nothing more I can do. Nothing anyone can do," looking at me, trying to see if I was getting the message but what kind of message was that? Like on the cop shows, when they say *Our hands are tied* and "If I were his friend," said Mr. Snell, as someone ran, laughing, down the hall, someone else running after, yelling *You geek! Give it back!* "—if I were his friend, I'd get him in to see Mr. Koss. Especially if there's been any kind of intimidation. Because Mr. Koss is all over things like that."

"OK," I said. "OK, thanks," and I hitched up my back-pack, turned to go but "Wait a minute," said Mr. Snell, and followed me to the door, turned the handle and "Get it back to me by Friday," he said, and put the form into my hand, canary-yellow paper, *What are you doing?* but then I saw them, down where the hallway splits: Magnur and Josh Winston, they didn't seem to be looking my way, but "Friday," Mr. Snell said again, loud enough to be overheard— and then, very quietly, "Let me know what happens, OK?"

"OK," and I took the paper, thinking *My locker, can I get there without having to pass them? or can I just not go there at all?* but the answer to both questions was no, my coat was in my locker, not to mention my house keys, and anyway, how big a coward was I willing to be? Once you give in there's no stopping the slide, so I kept walking, my footsteps not loud or quiet, walking toward them, walking past and *See*, with relief, *you're just being paranoid, they weren't even there for you at all—*

—but then "Hey, Justin," Josh Winston called. "Seen your Butt Boy lately?"

Smiling as he said it, almost laughing, but Magnur didn't smile, just looked at me, a flat look without any feeling at all. Then he started walking, so Josh Winston had to follow, walking backwards a pace behind and "Ask him," Josh Winston said, "ask him how he liked the—" *something*, I couldn't hear the last part and then they were turning the corner, they were gone—

—and I stood there, heart pounding, yellow form forgotten, *ask him how he liked the—*what?

And then I ran.

Ten

"He said," to Jinsen, opening Cokes for us both, "that Koss would be all over it. He said, 'If there's any kind of intimidation—' "

"No," soft and slow; he wiped again at the corner of his mouth, still leaking pink stuff, saliva and blood. "I don't think so."

"He has to, Jinsen! He's the Terminator, that's his *job*—"

"No," as soft and calm, maddeningly calm, tissue down and reaching for his brush because he was working, painting like it was just any day, every day but it wasn't every day that people ran you down and caught you out behind the parking lots, past the maintenance building where no one could see. . . . He wouldn't tell me what they did to him, but his mouth was swollen, his jaw was red, his T-shirt wrenched and torn and "They're *serious*," I said; I could hear my voice shaking—why? Anger? Fear? Fear for who? "They're not going to stop."

"They're *pretas*," lifting and dipping and trailing the brush, a wild magenta along the lion's back, nodding at me in this stupid optimistic way, like he wanted to believe somehow in human nature, like McManus and those guys were going to suddenly recognize the error of their ways, reform and say *Gosh, hey, we're sorry we hate you* . . . and for a second's flash I could almost see why they wanted to hit him, he was so stubborn, like a rock, what else can you use on a rock but dynamite? "It's like a cold," he said, switching from magenta to a silvery green. "It'll go away by itself if you let it run its course."

"No, it won't. It's a, a virus. Viruses just keep coming back." The Coke burned in my empty stomach, like the anger burning in my head and "Listen," I said, leaning forward; I plucked the brush from his hands. Even though I had my doubts about Mr. Valente, friend of the jocks, there was something so grim about Koss that you had to trust him, Koss didn't like *anybody* so "I'll go with you," I said, "OK? I'll tell Koss what I saw, what I know, and you—"

"No," at once, shaking his head, "no, *don't*, I don't want—"

"We have to! We can't just—"

And from behind us, "Michael?" a small high voice to startle us both, the brush fell from my hand, silver-green smeared on the table as "Aunty," Jinsen said, on a breath. "I didn't hear you come in."

More hat and coat than person, the tiny old great-aunt, and "Let me help you," Jinsen said, as she worked stiff fingers on the toggles of her coat, a kind of parka at least two sizes too big.

"I'm early today," she said. "The car service came at four, not four-thirty, I barely got into Dr. Bismack's—"

"Pretty soon I'll have my license," Jinsen said; his voice was very gentle. "Then you won't have to depend on them anymore."

"We'll have to get that old van fixed. It needs a starter, or an alternator, I don't remember what they said at the garage. . . ." Looking at me the way a kid would, shy peep behind the smeary glasses, and "This is my great-aunt Lily," Jinsen said. "Aunty, this is Justin. We're in Art together at school."

"Hello, Justin," still shy, letting Jinsen take her coat from her, kissing him on the cheek but then "Your face," she said, and touched his mouth; her smile sank and died. "What happened to your face?"

Jinsen didn't say anything.

"Were you, you weren't fighting again, were you? Oh, *Michael*," with such sorrow that I stared, I couldn't help it: Jinsen? *fighting?*

"No," he said at once, holding her hand, making her look at him. "I got hit. But I wasn't fighting, Aunty, I promise."

She touched his mouth again, her own lips trembling, as if she were about to cry and "Justin," Jinsen said, still in that calm gentle way, "wait for me in my room, OK?" So I did, sitting on the Army cot because there was no place else to sit, trying not to listen to the voices outside: hers high and scared and quavery, *Oh Michael, you promised!* and his calm *Don't worry,* over and over again, *Aunty, don't worry,* until she said something I couldn't hear, still upset but getting better and "—later, OK?" from Jinsen, right outside the door. "And I'll bring you some tea in a minute."

Inside, he shut the door behind him, then just stood there, breathing in and out, in and out in a rhythm I could see, his chest expanding, relaxing, until "OK," he said, and sat down, back straight, legs crossed, on the exercise mat. "You heard that much, you might as well hear the rest."

———

At the door, the house so quiet around us, his great-aunt somewhere upstairs and "See you tomorrow," Jinsen said; he sounded very tired. The bruises were showing now, dark smudge prints on his jaw, his neck, like time-lapse stains and "Maybe," I said, pulling on my gloves, "maybe you should put some ice on that, or something?"

He smiled, a lopsided smile with his swollen lips. "You don't ice a bruise."

"What do you do, then?"

"You ignore it."

There was plenty of ice on the seat of my bike, ice too on the driveway, on the curves and the corners, it took all my attention just to hold the road and that was good because I didn't want to think, just then, think about problems with no solutions, about everything Jinsen had told me—but still it echoed in my mind, what he'd said and the way he'd said it, with a smile I'd never seen before: self-mocking, cold, unkind, it didn't belong on his face and *I transferred here from upstate,* he'd said. *From Romney. It was like—you know that little metal basket in the drain, where all the garbage collects? That's Romney.*

By then there was no place left for him to go, he'd been through school after school, suspended then expelled for *prohibited behaviors,* he said, with that same un-Jinsen smile: thug stuff, like breaking into lockers, wrecking equipment in the gym, harassing people, *but most of all fighting. I fought, like, all the time. Big guys, little guys, didn't matter. I'd take anybody.*

Why?

Because I liked it, without a smile. *Because it was fun for me.*

Fun? like I couldn't believe it, I *couldn't* believe it, how could Jinsen be saying this? and *Once*, still unsmiling, *I cornered this kid in the library and I hit him in the face with a book. It was some kind of reference book, a big square book and I just kept hitting, and hitting, till the cover bent up in my hands—*

What happened to the kid?

I don't know.

Silence: the Buddha above us floating on in the blue; and Jinsen just looking at me, a calm and steady gaze, no excuses, no denials, until finally *Why?* I'd said, even though I knew it wasn't the right question.

I don't know, still calm. *It made me feel better, you know? Not good, but better. Like making stuff happen and then keeping it going, like a whirlpool or a tornado or something, keeping it swirling and boiling and all the while you're in the center, the eye of it, just watching. . . . It was— fun.*

And after the fights came the offices: vice-principal, principal, therapist, shrink, he'd been on meds and off them, in counseling and out, his father unforgiving—*I wash my hands of you*—while his mother tried everything, tried to find a school he could stick with, a therapy that would change him, quit her job to stay home with him, offered to move to another city if that would maybe help. *She said she would do anything,* looking not at me but at the ceiling, the painted clouds, the white sun of the light fixture. *Anything that would help me. And she did.*

Did what?

She died.

He'd skipped school that day, like a million other days, doing nothing, hanging out until he was out of money, he had to come home: to find the house empty, both his parents gone, they stayed gone but *I didn't even know,* he'd said, *until the next morning. This lady from Social Services came, and*—and then he hadn't said anything else, just sat there, breathing in and out as I wondered what it must be like, to come home to a silence that never breaks, an endless silence echoed endlessly inside and *The guy who ran into them,* still looking up at the light, *it was like his fifth offense, DUI, the judge was really mad* and so the guy went to prison, and Jinsen went to a treatment center because he wouldn't talk, wouldn't move, wouldn't blink his eyes, *it's called catatonia* and he stayed that way for almost a month, a lifetime until *Kim came,* Kim the art teacher who taught him how to use a pencil and a brush, who taught him about Buddhism, about the Four Noble Truths—

Remembering what my dad had said, the bodhi tree, the Four Noble Truths and *What's that? I'd asked. Like the Golden Rule?*

Kind of, yeah. Mostly it's about doing no harm, to people, animals, cockroaches, everybody. Even to yourself.

It was Kim who gave him his new name, "Jinsen," meaning "the fountain of God, the place where God springs up in the world" and *Kim told me everything,* he'd said, still staring into the light. *How to paint, how to sleep at night, how to talk to my mom again, by praying. . . . And he knew about the whirlpool, about wanting to—stir things up. Because it calms you down. But he showed me a different way. . . . It wasn't shaving his head, you know, or chanting that made him a Buddhist: it was who he was. Kim was so—he was an open hand, right? open to everybody. But strong, too, really strong, no one could make him do anything he didn't want to do. And I wanted to be that way, too.*

Finally Kim started talking about the fighting, about bouncing from school to school, about who Michael Martin was and who Jinsen could be and *That's why I understand McManus. Because I used to be him, kind of. A hungry ghost.*

With a god inside.

He'd smiled then, a real Jinsen smile. *With a god inside.*

Which is why I was finally able to stop, right? And why I don't fight anymore. . . . I promised Kim, I promised—my mom. And I'm not going to talk to the Enforcer or the Terminator or whatever you called him, and you aren't either. Because if I do or you do, there'll just be more crap from McManus. And I am not going to fight.

The bike tires juddered as I tried to brake; I held on, got the bike to stop, let my feet drag in the mud and slush. Audrey's car was in the driveway, ticking, still warm; warm lights in the living room, in the kitchen, bright and inviting and safe and "Hey," I said to Audrey at the counter, busy slicing tomatoes, red seeds, silver knife. "You need some help with anything?"

She gave me a look, eyebrows up like *What's all this about?* but for once asked no questions: "You can set the table," she said, so I did, napkins, silverware, water glasses, thinking of Jinsen's parents, of his mother, of Kim, until "What lousy weather," Audrey said, glancing out the window, the shivering rivers of wet. "I can hardly believe it's almost spring."

Spring, spring break, *Can I bring him with me?* but I'd forgotten to ask him, forgotten all about it, I'd have to ask him "Soon," I said, and took my seat at the table, watching the rain on the windows as if I'd never seen it before.

Eleven

"But if you can't really play," said Mr. Freeberg, arms raised, like he was praying, or calling down an air strike, "then why did you audition for the role of the Fiddler?"

"Well, you know, I can play *some*—"

" 'Some' is right," Jakob's murmur, not a FuBar today but a bag of organic corn chips, passing them back and forth, we were trying hard to be quiet but "Whoever's *rattling* out there," Freeberg snarled, "please quit it," so we got up and moved to the very back, even warmer here than the rest of the dim auditorium, warm enough to start a sweat and "I heard," Jakob said, "that they really messed Jinsen up. True?"

"His neck is bruised," I said. "But that's mostly it."

"Then why wasn't he at school today? I didn't see him in the cafeteria—"

"He went to CAC, with Snell," to meet with Ed Keeley, the one who'd commissioned the banner, both of them supposed to be back in time for Art where I'd hear all about it, ask about spring break too and "He may be kind of—odd," Jakob said, "but he's definitely got some balls. I wouldn't like to go one-on-one with McManus and his merry men. Especially Cro-Magnur."

"Me either," I said, and felt a sudden rush of pride, pride in Jinsen, who wasn't afraid of McManus or Magnur, *big guys, little guys, didn't matter, I'd take anybody*—and strangely proud, too, to be his friend, like being friends with the Dalai Lama or, or Jesus, or someone like that. Someone who could hit back, but wouldn't, someone really—good.

"Can you *pretend* to play, then? along with a soundtrack? Like lip-synching?"

"Lip sink?" and "I have to go," I said, out to the aisle as quietly as I could, careful not to let the big door bang behind me. Lunch was almost over anyway, time for Econ; as I headed for my locker I thought about Jinsen at CAC, *wonder what it's like there, wonder if he's—*

"Hey," in my way, some big body I tried by instinct to sidestep but "Wait a minute," Magnur in a bulky blue jacket, one hand out, not touching me; yet. "I want to talk to you."

My heart jumped, a ragged rhythm; I could taste the chips in my throat, a salty, pulpy taste, and "Come here," as he turned, to lead me away from the auditorium, lead me where? to some blind hall somewhere, where he could hand me my head? "No," I said, trying to sound calm, to sound like Jinsen would. *Hungry ghosts*, remember, Magnur's just a hungry ghost. "You want to talk, let's talk right here."

A deep scowl, arms folded but "OK," he said, hard, "let's talk. About your friend Buddha Boy." A few people passed, glanced, kept on going; cowards. I didn't blame them. " 'Cause he's really your friend. I know."

A thought went through me, fleeting and dark—*No he's not, not really, we just hang out sometimes*—and "Yeah," I said; my voice was all in my throat now, tight and hollow, defiant. "He's my friend. So what?"

"So why?"

"What?"

"I said *why*," furious, like I was deliberately playing dumb. "Why do you hang out with him? Why do you stick up for him? The kid's a freak, he doesn't even belong here." I opened my mouth, but he wasn't done; in a weird way it was like he wasn't even talking to me, but to Jinsen some-how *through* me, like I was a translator, a gateway. "He wears freak clothes, he acts like a freak, he sure *talks* like a freak—"

"Well, ignore him," my voice a little better, a little stronger, but not much. "Just, just pretend he's not—"

"Ignore him! How can you ignore him? You know what he said to me yesterday? when he, when we were— He said, 'If it makes you happy.' That's what he said. 'Go on, if it makes you happy.' What the hell is that supposed to mean?" Yelling now, but again not at me: it was as if he were arguing with Jinsen, arguing with himself, his face get-ting redder and redder and "You tell him," poking me in the chest, big fat hot-dog finger, "tell him to stay the hell away from me. Just tell him that."

Stomping off as I stood there, as the bell went, as I walked slowly down the emptied halls to get a late slip, as I sat in Econ to wait for Art where the first person I saw was Jinsen, bruised neck, big smile and "Wait'll you hear," he said but "Wait'll *you* hear," as Megan, silent, stared at us both. "About my nice little lunchtime chat with Magnur," and I told him all about it, red face, hot-dog finger and all and after a pause, his pause "Maybe it doesn't," Jinsen said.

"Maybe what doesn't what?"

"Make him happy. Beating people up, maybe it doesn't

really—" and "Guys," Snell said, knuckle-tapping on our table, *knock-knock*. "Go on and get your blocks," to make wood-block prints, that day's assignment, big white sheets and little troughs of ink but my mind wasn't on it, especially after Jinsen told me his news: he'd been offered a summer internship at CAC, a chance to study painting with Ed Kee-ley, "depending, you know, on how he likes the banner." Working the block in the ink, how could he be so calm about it? If it were me, I'd be jumping up and down: Ed Keeley for a teacher! As a sophomore!

"So what'd you tell him?" I said. "What'd you *say*?"

"I said," mild, "that I hoped he liked the banner. —Hey, you're getting stuff all over Megan," which I was, ink splashes on her lime-green sleeve, tiny black raindrops and "Justin, you *slob*!" in a shriek that turned heads but I didn't pay attention, I was still watching Jinsen: calm gaze and careful hands, no wasted motion, working on his print as if it were any day, as if yesterday's bad news or the great news today were all just . . . part of everything, and he was just taking everything as it came, how could he do that? How could he keep *on* doing that? Balls? Luck? Karma?

The kid's a freak.

The fountain of God, the place where God springs up in the world.

His print was awesome, by the way.

Twelve

The flyers were up all over the place, in Rucher red and black: THE PRIDE OF RUCHER, BE THERE, ANNUAL PRIDE ASSEMBLY for all the usual suspects, the future valedictorians and the All-State jocks, shiny gold plaques and the school orchestra playing the school fight song, "Pride of the Lions," as the rest of us sat and clapped like trained seals. *Gosh I'm just so glad Mark McManus got another award, aren't you? Oh my goodness yes, he can never have too many.* "What a shuck it all is," I said to Jinsen, stepping sideways over a puddle. "I'd rather watch a hundred Econ videos than sit through that swill one more time."

"Well," pausing to readjust his backpack, his giant shirt ruffled by the breeze, "why shouldn't they get honored?

They do good stuff, right? Get straight A's, win a bunch of games—"

"I don't care; it's boring. They could at least pick someone different for a change."

We were walking home, on a day finally more spring than winter, chirping birds and actual sun, snow lumps melted down to visible grass, heading this time to my house because the banner was pretty much finished, only minor touch-ups left to do, nothing I could even pretend to help with. So today we were going to look through art books, Picasso and Klee and Monet, all the stuff I'd gotten from my dad and "He's working on a new piece now," I said. "It's black-and-white and big as a car, he says. . . . You know, I'm going to visit him for spring break. Would you—do you want to come with?"

"To your dad's studio, you mean? Really?" and he smiled, a big smile, we both did, but then "For a whole week?" he said; his smile dwindled. "My great-aunt—I don't know."

"You mean she'll say no?" That wavery smile, *Oh Michael*, she didn't seem like the bossy type but "She can check it out with my dad first. Or he could call her—"

"No, I mean I don't know if I can leave her on her own for that long. Maybe if someone came to check, made sure she was OK—"

93

I almost volunteered Audrey, *Hey, my mom could do it,* but then I thought I ought to ask her first. Still, "Do you always have to, to worry about that stuff?" I asked, as we turned down my street, winding sidewalks beneath elms bare-branched to show last year's birds' nests, squirrels' nests, winter-worn but still intact. The dalmatian on the corner sniffed through his redwood gate, then barked as we passed, a sharp fierce noise, *strangers!* "It's not fair to you, why can't she just—"

"She's old," he said, which wasn't really an answer but somehow it shut me up, because it was true, she *was* old, old and frail, we walked along in silence until "Your street," he said, as we turned up the driveway. "All the trees, and everything. . . . It's nice."

He thought our house was nice, too, nice and big, which compared to his I guess it was, but I'd stopped seeing his house as small, or shabby, especially his room, which made mine look like a dumping ground for "King Consumer," too much junk piled way too high, stuff I never used or didn't need, or even really want. It was strange, as if I were seeing through his eyes, like catching a glimpse of myself in a mirror, a mirror I didn't know was there.

"How about some herbal tea?" Audrey asked, Audrey who followed us into the kitchen, Audrey who seemed to like Jinsen instantly. "Or oolong, I have oolong," like *shaved head and dragon shirt* must equal *tea drinker*, no stereotypes there.

"We'll just have Cokes," I said, annoyed—until I saw Jinsen's smile, smiling at Audrey, almost wistful and *His mom*, I thought. *She's gone.*

"Tea's good, too," I said.

We spent a while going through the art books—he liked Picasso best, the blunt bent faces, the force behind the brush—but Jinsen looked longest at my dad's painting, looked and touched, one finger gentle on the whorls and flecks of paint. "I don't use oils," he said, "yet. Mostly I do acrylics. . . . Does your dad ever sell his paintings?"

"Not a lot; sometimes. He says he sells just enough to buy the paint to do more."

I picked up my cup, the tea was cold and "When my parents died," Jinsen said, looking down at the painting in his hands, "there was a settlement, and insurance money too, I guess. My great-aunt had it put in some kind of trust, like for when I'm twenty-one. But some of it," red and green, red and green, tracing the circle around, "she gave to me. And that's what I spent it on."

I thought of the tackle box, the paints and brushes. "All of it?"

95

"All of it. She told me it was mine and I should do whatever I thought was best. So I thought, what would Kim do with it? And then I knew. . . . Kim always told me I ought to go to art school."

"Well, once you get that internship, you—"

"Who knows if I'll get it? If Keeley doesn't like the banner—"

"How can he not like it? It's great, it's—the lion looks alive, all of it is alive—" in spring green and crimson and smoky gray, ideograms like water flowing beneath, STUDENTS OF ASIA AT CAC, and "If he hasn't gone blind," I said, "he'll see how great it is."

"Maybe," he said, and shrugged, but in that moment his face, his gaze, was so still that I could see all the way to the bottom, like looking into a deep clear pond, and what I saw there was a longing so intense that it startled me, a want that was a need, like needing food or air. "I did my best," he said, and looked away. "I just wish I'd had that other scroll to show him, too."

"Don't worry," I said; because I knew, I was sure. "The banner will be enough."

And then "Knock knock," from Audrey, opening the door a crack. "Jinsen, would you like to stay for dinner? I'm making chicken stew," and "Sure," he said, head turned to smile up at her; suddenly he seemed younger, almost like a kid. "Sure, thanks."

Audrey outdid herself with the meal—stew, fresh-baked rolls, corn on the cob—and Jinsen ate everything she put on the table, thanking her again and again. During dinner she asked her usual million questions—what kind of music did he listen to, did he play any sports, how did he like school (I had to roll my eyes at that one)—but to Jinsen, I guess, it didn't seem intrusive. Maybe he liked having a mom give him the friendly third degree, even if it wasn't his mom.

He ended up staying till almost nine o'clock, I wondered what his great-aunt would say but "It's Tuesday," he said to me, as Audrey searched for her car keys. "Tuesday nights she goes to bingo with our neighbor. . . . Thanks again," to Audrey, "for driving me home."

"Oh, it's no trouble at all. Do you have your coat?" which made me cringe a little, but "Well," Jinsen said, past the closing door, "the thing with that is—"

I cleared up the dinner stuff and loaded the dishwasher, as a way to say thank you to Audrey. She didn't come back right away, and when she did I was ready for some more *Oh that poor boy* no-jacket stuff, but "What a sweet family," she said; her voice was soft, almost sad, but in a good way, the way it is when something you see touches you, moves

97

your heart inside. "Jinsen is quite a remarkable young man. And his great-aunt is just adorable—"

"You met her?"

"Only for a minute. —You know," hanging up her coat, "your father mentioned that you were asking Jinsen along to his place, for vacation. Do you think his great-aunt might need a little help while he's gone? Just someone looking in, stopping by for a cup of tea or something. . . . I would have suggested it myself, but I didn't want to seem pushy."

"I don't think it would be pushy at all," I said, with a little smile; the tickle of karma again? "I think it would be nice."

Thirteen

We ended up sitting right in front, Jakob and Megan and me, two rows back from the stage where the honorees were already displayed before the red-and-black curtains, under the Rucher logo: suits and dresses in a double row of folding chairs, jocks on the right side, brains on the left and "LaRonda says," Megan's murmur, "that when she gets *her* plaque she's going to stand up and make a speech. 'I want to thank the *Academy*, I want to thank Mr. *Valente*—' "

" 'And Mr. *Koss*,' " I said, " 'for not catching me smoking every day in the parking lot.' "

" 'And all the little people, who sit in front of me in Art.'—Hey, Justin," Jakob poking me, "how come Jinsen's up there?" by the stairway side of the curtains, bright red shirt and talking to Snell, why? and "I don't know," I said, "he didn't—"

But then the orchestra started up, *dum-dum-DEE* with kettle drums and all, like we were at a coronation or something and "Welcome to our Pride of Rucher assembly," Mr. Valente front and center with the mike: dark suit, salt-and-pepper hair, he looks like he ought to be a politician. In a way, I guess, he already is. "We have a lot to be proud of today, so let's get started."

Two senior girls in sparkly black were in charge of the plaques; they waited in front of Jinsen and Snell, moving forward every time another name was called, names I could have called without the list: LaRonda, Caitlin Driver, Aaron Hitaka, Chelsea Sweet, Josh Winston, Darren Magnur—

"He looks like the Minotaur in that suit, doesn't he?" Megan was doing Greek mythology this semester. "Half man, half cow—"

"Half bull, you mean," said Jakob.

"Bull is right," I said, watching how Magnur never looked once at Jinsen, who smiled and clapped for him the same way he did for everybody, for Josh Winston, even for McManus, who got two awards: one for Outstanding Student Athlete and one for Student Leadership—student *leadership*, can you believe it? And as McManus crossed the stage the second time—nice suit, modest smile, picture-perfect on the outside—I wanted to yell, or boo, or *something*. I couldn't bear his smug disgusting smile, or the people around me applauding how he looked, not what they knew he was: it was so backwards, it was so *Rucher*, but *hungry ghosts*, I told myself, and though I didn't clap—nothing on earth could have made me clap—I didn't yell out either, just sat there with my arms folded, a couple of people looked sideways at me but by then I was looking at Jinsen, serene at the side of the stage, Snell was crossing to the microphone and "We have a special award today," he said, "for a very special student. He hasn't been here at Rucher for very long, but we think he epitomizes the best of our student body, combining talent with determination to produce something extraordinary—" as the red-and-black curtains began to move, "—that represents Rucher in a special way—"

—and you could hear it, like a wave, a sound wave rushing through the crowd, *oooh* as the banner came into view: spring green and crimson, silver ribbons dangling from each side, and the lion triumphant, filling the wall, its painted eyes gleaming, amazingly alive and "—commissioned by the Creative Arts Center, chosen for a special award—Jinsen Martin," as the girls in black led Jinsen forward; he was shorter than both of them, he looked like a hobo at a fancy dress ball. And he was smiling, a wide shy happy smile, as Snell stopped clapping long enough to shake his hand—

—and I caught his eye as he took his plaque, and I was smiling, too, no, I was grinning, hands above my head—

—as on either side of me Megan and then Jakob started clapping too, the three of us in rhythm, *Jin-sen Jin-sen*

—and onstage, Caitlin Driver joined our rhythm, and then LaRonda, and then the whole stage was clapping, even Magnur, still not looking at Jinsen, the whole auditorium applauding

—even McManus, cold and polite, like a robot, he would do the perfect thing, wouldn't he? but I didn't care about him, I didn't care about anything but seeing Jinsen below his banner, snow lion triumphant and *Karma*, I thought, *this is his karma, his reward for being who he is.*

Afterwards, I made my way to the stage, Jakob and Megan came too but it seemed like everyone wanted to talk to him now: Caitlin and LaRonda and the senior girls in black, Mr. Snell saying something in his ear but finally "Hey," as he left the stage, plaque tucked under his arm. "So why didn't you tell me?"

"I didn't know, not about this," tapping the plaque. "Mr. Snell said, Let's hang the banner for the assembly, but—"

"It's a *great* banner," said Megan, looking him right in the eye.

"So now you're a star," Jakob said, and we all laughed, not because it was funny but because we felt like laughing, we felt good. "Now you go to CAC," I said, "and you get your internship, and—"

"We'll see," and he shrugged. "He hasn't seen the banner yet," as we stepped around a crowd in the aisle, congratulating Chelsea Sweet, Josh Winston. "Snell's going to take it over there this afternoon, right after school . . . He wants me to go, too."

In the hallway, we passed the other banner: little black lions, RUCHER CAN'T <u>SUCCEED</u> WITHOUT <u>U</u>! and "Looks kind of dull now," I said, "doesn't it? Kind of small?"

"They ought to replace it with yours," Megan said.

Jakob peered over his glasses. "Actually," he said, "Rucher also can't <u>suck</u> without <u>U</u>," and we all laughed again.

———

The rest of the day flowed on in a pleasant haze. At lunchtime the cafeteria ladies gave Jinsen a freebie, his pick of anything (he chose the veggie pizza); Caitlin Driver came up again to say hi and talk about painting; no one threw pennies. At the play rehearsal the banner still hung over the stage, and I sat there wondering how he'd managed that trick of perspective, how hanging it up on the wall made it come so totally alive. I thought, *I bet my dad would know.*

Below it, onstage, the play went on, Megan glowering, stopped again and again by Freeberg: "This isn't improv, Megan, you're not allowed to change your lines—"

"But it's what *Golde* would really *say*!"

She was still grumbling about it in Art, while we sketched our still life (still lives?), two eggs and a crooked daisy, and "Freeberg," she said, "is *stifling* my creativity. . . . Jinsen," demanding, "does CAC have *acting* classes?"

His pencil paused; he gave me half a smile. "I don't know."

"Well, *find out*, will you? when you go there today? Because Freeberg—" and on and on, high drama-queen mode, she hadn't even drawn one egg before the bell went and "Let me know what happens," I said to Jinsen. "Even though I know what's going to happen."

"OK," he said, seemed about to say more but "Jinsen," from Snell, "come here a second," and as he turned away I felt—I don't know, not sad exactly but kind of at a loss: because the afternoons working on the banner were over, because things were changing, because even good change means something has to go. But afterwards, as Megan and I went one way and he went another, heading upstairs to his locker: "Later," Jinsen called down, "I'll tell you everything," which made me feel better, like not everything was changing after all.

We had to go back to get Jakob, who was arguing grades with his Civics teacher, Mrs. Jimms, who everybody called Slim Jimms because she was fat and "Why should I care," his frown in the hall, "about the stupid branches of government? I'm not planning on running for President any time soon."

"You think *that's* bad, what about what *Freeberg*—"

"Meg, come on, give it a rest, OK?" but she kept on complaining all the way to the car, her turn to drive but "Now I can't even find my *keys*!" so we had to sit there while she searched her purse, why do girls have to carry so much stuff around? Makeup and pencils and squished-up tissue, but no keys there or in her backpack, or her coat pockets, now she was seriously mad.

"I can't *believe* this, I just *had* them—" but the last time she actually remembered having them was at rehearsal so "I'll check backstage," as she and I recrossed the parking lot, Jakob waiting by the car, "and you can check the— *Hey*," to some people coming out, Hooks and Josh Winston, "hey, hold the *door*!" because it was a crashbar door, it locks automatically if you let it swing shut.

Which they did, of course. "Oh thanks a *lot*!" and Josh

Winston laughed, a rushed little chuckle like he was out of breath, he and Hooks pushed right through me and Megan—

—as the door swung open again, right back at us, Megan hopping backwards into me: as McManus hurried out, he didn't even see us but I saw him, saw the look on his face and that look was all—darkness, the opposite of his perfect stage face, his real self cold and satisfied—

—by what? what was going on? but "Come *on*," Megan snapped, tugging my arm. "Now we have to go around—" to the other door, the maintenance door, she knew her way down the cramped little hall but I had to stumble after her, scared now, scared of what?

And suddenly lights burst on, bright white overheads and someone was there, some guy grabbing my arm, Freeberg and "Got him!" he yelled, really yelled, I'd never heard him like that before.

"You just stand *still*," to me, shaking my shoulder, shaking it hard as Snell came around the corner, white-faced and "No," he said when he saw me, "no, that's not him—"

—as Megan, somewhere close by, made a sound, a small choked cry and I broke away from Freeberg, blundering through the weight of the curtains to see Jinsen there, staring up, staring over my head at the banner, his beautiful banner—

—now hanging limp and desecrated, half-ripped from the wall, its writing fouled by footprints, its ribbons gone—and the lion, the lion was the worst, slashed and gutted like a live thing murdered.

And "What happened?" from one of the janitors, rushing down the long main aisle as Freeberg turned to yell at him: "Where were you?"

"I was just outside! Some kid asked me—"

"—supposed to be security—"

"—for help, what was I—oh *man*," finally seeing the banner, seeing Snell with his face like iron, Megan crying, hands hanging at her sides—

—and Jinsen, staring, his eyes like slits, and if I had seen into his eyes before, seen the clean longing like a reflection in a pool, now the water was muddy, stained by a sick black slurry, he looked like a stranger, he looked like . . . McManus. "Jinsen," I said, loud, as if calling him back from a cliff. "Jinsen!"

But he didn't turn, didn't move, just kept staring as if he were alone in the room so I put my face right in his face, to make him see me, make him hear, and "Jinsen!" hands on his arms, "don't! You hear me? Just *don't.*"

And he blinked at me then, a sluggish blink like a lizard's eye: but I knew he'd heard, I squeezed his arms and "Wait," I said, "wait here—" and then went past him, to where if I

107

stretched my full height I could touch the dangling shreds of the banner, touch the lion's clawed face—

—and I pulled it down, the pieces I could gather, then jumped offstage and started up the aisle. No one tried to stop me: Freeberg was still yelling at the janitor, Snell and Megan beside Jinsen who stood there like a statue, as if he had gone back inside himself, deep inside where no one else could go.

And then I was pushing at the auditorium door, I heard it bang behind me, far behind because now I was moving faster, striding, running down the halls with the dead lion in my arms

depending on how he likes the banner

I know what's going to happen

what always happens, it never stops, the ones like Mc-Manus do whatever the hell they want and no one sees it, no one cares

but not this time, not anymore

and someone calling to me, at me, some teacher shouting "Hey!" but I kept on going, pounding feet and pounding heart, running till my foot slipped and I crashed into the wall, shoulder numb but I scrambled up again, I kept on because now I knew where I was going: around the corner, into the cafeteria hall where I slipped again and fell even harder this time, hard enough to take my breath, I lay for a second on the shiny floor gasping like a fish on the sand

and saw hanging above me the bloodred banner, RUCHER CAN'T <u>SUCCEED</u> WITHOUT <u>U</u>!

not anymore

so I crawled upright to rip it down, fling it away like the lie that it was, then fixed the pieces of Jinsen's banner to the brackets instead, Jinsen's lion, its ruined proud beautiful face

as around the corner came Valente, Valente and Koss, they stopped dead when they saw me and "What're you doing?" Valente said, Koss advancing on me but "He did this!" my hands in fists now, my voice a roar, "McManus did this and you let him! You ▬▬▬▬ *let* him, day after day after day! But not anymore! Not anymore!"

And I kicked at the pieces of the fallen banner like I was kicking at McManus, at Rucher, at every time they'd looked the other way, all of them, all of us, I tried to kick Koss, too, when he put his hands on me—but all he did was hold me still, until I stopped kicking, until I stood with my face pressed against the wall, beside the lion's eyes.

Fourteen

So explain this, now: You wish, want, work for one thing, but instead something else happens, the thing you most dreaded, the thing you tried your best to stop. And then it turns out that what you wanted, all you wanted and more, stood hidden behind exactly what you didn't, and to get to one you had to take the other first.

Is that how life goes? Is that how life is *supposed* to go— like walking blindfolded and backwards to get to where you need to be? Or is it just karma, gods and lions and hungry ghosts, doing what it has to do?

Slanting bands of afternoon light, filmy with the dust she'd kicked up sweeping and "Oh, I *hate* you," Megan said, poking Jinsen's shoulder with the handle of the broom. "How can you make your lines go so *straight*?"

"It's a Zen thing," said Jakob.

"I just measure," said Jinsen, dipping the brush again.

Afternoon, after school, the four of us in the art room and "Thanks again," Snell said, "for helping," helping straighten up, put away supplies, clear the decks before we all went off for break. Megan and her mom were headed to Mexico, Jakob was staying home "to sleep, just sleep, fourteen wonderful hours a day," and Jinsen and I were going to my dad's so *I have to finish*, he'd said, finish touching up the piece he was making, this cool little painting, black-and-white like an abstract grid—because after today he wouldn't be in the art room anymore, he wouldn't be at Rucher anymore. Jinsen was transferring to CAC.

Karma: that's the only way I can explain it. After they peeled me off the wall, and I finally told what I knew—from what had happened to the banner to the campaign of persecution, the ruined sketchbook, the daily penny-toss, the way they'd ganged up on Jinsen in the parking lot—Koss went into true Terminator mode, shaking down witnesses, calling parents, the whole deal. McManus's parents had a hard time believing that their Mark could be anything less than wonderful, let alone such an evil shit, but Koss hung tough and suspended him anyway, for harassment. And the whole thing got written up in his record—his perfect Student Leadership permanent record—so that was something, at least. And he and Magnur had a big shouting match in the gym, so maybe that was something, too.

I wish I could say that the rest of the crew were expelled, or run out of town by an angry mob, or something, but what did happen was that Hooks and Josh Winston had to do three days' worth of school maintenance to make up for destroying school property, which mostly meant humping trash in the cafeteria, where people could see them and make garbageman jokes. Which everyone did. Except for Jinsen.

Who seemed the same as ever, cross-legged on his bedroom floor beneath the mended banner, its scraps pieced together like battle scars, like it had fought with something big and cruel, and won. *Valente was pretty cool*, he'd told me. *He and Snell really went all out to get me in. Snell told Keeley about the first scroll, and showed my sketchbook.*

I wish I'd said something before, I said, not looking at him. *I wish I'd done something—*

You did, Jinsen quiet in the quiet of his room. *If it wasn't for you, I might have—gone after McManus. I wanted to.*

I know. But I didn't really—

Yes you did, nodding, twice and slow. *You said, "Don't."*

As the story filtered through school, things changed a little, in those last few weeks before break. Not that people started hating McManus—I wish—but at least they stopped hassling Jinsen, they acted normal if not outright nice but that was, what do you call it? a moot point, it didn't matter anymore because he was just about gone already, reaching escape velocity with every dab of the brush. "You want to come over after school?" I asked him now in the art room, but he couldn't, he had to go see Ed Keeley with Snell, but "I'll see you in the morning," he said. "For the trip, right?"

"Right," I said, and turned away, back to stacking chairs, blue and silver, slide and thump. It had been like this since he found out about the transfer: not that he was ditching me, but that he truly didn't have the time, so much now to get done—Rucher transcripts, CAC paperwork for his great-aunt to fill out, get together a portfolio. Because everything was different now. Because his life had changed.

Would it still have me in it? I didn't know; I don't think he knew, either, which made our spring break a kind of ghost trip, a memory in advance, last gasp of the good old days but they weren't good to me because two Mondays from now I'd be back in the grind, nothing changed except no Jinsen in Econ, no Jinsen in Art, no Jinsen after school because he'd be busy making new friends, artist friends, no time left for hanging out . . . so was I jealous? Of CAC, no: if anyone should be there it was Jinsen. Then was I really happy? Yes. And no.

Now from Megan "Where does the *paint* go?" with her hands heaped full, bent and shiny tubes and "On the paper," said Jakob, so she threw one at him, cadmium yellow, it hit me in the back and "OK," said Snell, tucking a folder in his desk. "I think we're all done here, guys."

All done: in paint and paper, black and white and "Hey Justin," Jinsen said, looking around for a towel, wiping his hands on his pants. "I was going to give this painting to your dad. Like a, a thank you for having me come and visit. You think he'd like it?"

Grid lines, running and blurring onto the paper's edges, all the way to infinity and gone. "Yeah," I said. "I know he would."

"And," reaching into his knobby backpack, grown now to twice its usual size, "this is for you." Holding out his sketchbook, wavy and watermarked. "Snell thinks I should use it for my portfolio," he said. "But I wanted you to have it. If you want it."

If I want it: his *sketchbook*? with its months of work, its perfect tree, the mud marks, the stains of memory—and he'd even signed it, there inside the cover, TO JUSTIN, FROM JINSEN in looping blue letters.

"Of course I want it," I said, and stood there stupid, trying to think how to thank him, to say something worthy of the gift but "Come on," from Snell behind us, "let's go," herding us toward the door, Megan and Jakob already waiting outside and "See you in the morning," Jinsen said to me, smiling, then turned away, holding the painting by its edges, careful of the wet, and walked down the hall with Snell.

———

"He gave me his sketchbook," I told my dad on the phone that night; why had I called him? He'd be there in the morning. "To keep, I mean."

"Wow. That's quite a gift, from an artist."

"Yeah. I know."

Silence, as if he expected me to say more, then when I didn't, "I'm figuring I should make it there by ten," he said. "You all packed and ready to go?"

"Yeah," again and slow, more silence until "You sound sad," my dad said.

I didn't say anything.

"Your mother told me that things worked out OK at school."

"They did. They worked out great," better than I could have planned . . . but I *was* sad, sad and somehow pissed at "Karma," I said, and mashed my pillow on my head, it felt selfish to say, to feel, but I said it anyway: "What about my karma? I tried to help, to do the right thing, and now I'm losing a friend. Is that fair?"

The hum of distance, like an unspoken thought and "No," my dad said. "It isn't. Did you think it would be?"

I didn't answer, just lay there listening: to nothing, his silence, the warm sound of my breath against cloth until finally "I'll see you tomorrow, kiddo," he said, and was gone into dial-tone drone, two-fingered knocking at my door, Audrey asking was I done with the phone so I handed it back, scrunched up my pillow to lie eyes-open, thinking of nothing, of CAC, of Jinsen's dumb T-shirts, of karma. Of how it's like a circle, like cause and effect: wavy lines and watermarks, bruises and darkness, a torn-up lion and hungry ghosts. And people getting what they really deserve. Eventually. Which might mean forever.

Because *we're all gods inside*, right? and always friends, every time I open his sketchbook, whether we see each other at school or not, or even ever again. Is that fair? *Did you think it would be?*

TO JUSTIN, FROM JINSEN.

On the next-to-last page was a drawing I hadn't seen before, a sketch he'd made of me: in Art, at our table, was it "our" table yet or still just mine and Megan's, and him exiled to one side? From the angle you couldn't tell, and to him I'm sure it didn't matter. In the drawing I'm working on something, intent, absorbed, and I look just like myself, only better. The way I was when I was with him; the way I really am, like his drawing of a tree *was* a tree? I don't know. How would I know that?

Use your eyes, my dad would say.

You want to see karma coming? Go look in the mirror, right now.

117